DIANA ANYAKWO grew up in Lagos, Nigeria. She is of mixed Irish and Nigerian heritage. She moved to the UK when she was a teenager and later graduated from the University of Manchester with a degree in Molecular Biology and a Masters in Bioreactor Systems. She spent three years in Athens, Greece where she taught English and worked as an editor at an educational publisher. She currently lives and works in Manchester as a freelance writer and editor of English Language teaching materials. She loves reading, writing and binge-watching TV series. She also loves going for long walks to help get inspiration for her writing.

T0349107

MY LIFE
AS A
CHAMELEON

DIANA ANYAKWO

ATOM

First published in the United Kingdom in 2023 by Atom

5 7 9 10 8 6 4

Copyright © Diana Anyakwo, 2023

The moral right of the author has been asserted.

*All characters and events in this publication, other than those
clearly in the public domain, are fictitious and any resemblance
to real persons, living or dead, is purely coincidental.*

All rights reserved.
No part of this publication may be reproduced, stored in a
retrieval system, or transmitted, in any form or by any means, without
the prior permission in writing of the publisher, nor be otherwise circulated
in any form of binding or cover other than that in which it is published
and without a similar condition including this condition being
imposed on the subsequent purchaser.

A CIP catalogue record for this book
is available from the British Library.

ISBN: 978-1-4721-5615-0

Printed and bound in Great Britain by
Clays Ltd, Elcograf S.p.A.

Papers used by Atom are from well-managed forests
and other responsible sources.

MIX
Paper | Supporting
responsible forestry
FSC® C104740

Atom
An imprint of
Little, Brown Book Group
Carmelite House
50 Victoria Embankment
London EC4Y 0DZ

The authorised representative
in the EEA is
Hachette Ireland
8 Castlecourt Centre
Dublin 15, D15 XTP3, Ireland
(email: info@hbgi.ie)

An Hachette UK Company
www.hachette.co.uk

www.littlebrown.co.uk

*In memory of Mum and Dad – you
mean everything to me and without
you I wouldn't be who I am today*

'I am not afraid of storms, for I am learning how to sail my ship.'

LOUISA MAY ALCOTT,
Little Women

AUTHOR'S NOTE

In my novel I have chosen to use the following terms that, while they may be uncomfortable to readers, are true to the background, experience and setting of the story and are not meant to cause offence.

Half-caste: When I was growing up in Nigeria in the 1970s, '80s and up until the early '90s people who had one Nigerian parent and one parent from a different race, usually white, were called half-caste by Nigerians. My family and other family friends all used the same word. We never felt it was derogatory or racist; it simply meant that in a majority black population we were half-white. To this day many people still use the term in Nigeria.

It wasn't until I came to the UK that I learnt that the term was considered offensive. I did some research online and discovered the origins of the term. It was used in the British colonial era in Asia, Africa and Australia to describe mixed race people. In Latin the word caste means pure and so half-caste means half-pure or impure. In Britain and Australia, the word half-caste was used as a racial slur for people of mixed heritage. In Nigeria, it was not considered a racial slur but merely a description of a person's race.

Nigerwife: This is a foreign woman married to a Nigerian man. The Nigerwives-Nigeria association (https://nigerwives. wixsite.com/nigeria) was set up in 1979 by a small group of foreign women married to Nigerian men and living in Nigeria to provide mutual support. At the time foreign women married to Nigerians encountered challenges with residence permits, work permits and re-entry visas. They also faced discrimination in the workplace, as they did not receive the same salary or benefits that expatriates did and were not entitled to the pension that applied to Nigerians. The association worked tirelessly to improve these conditions for Nigerwives and in 1999 the women were able to apply for Nigerian citizenship and receive the benefits and protection that provided. Many Nigerwives who married their partners before the 1980s were ostracized by their families in Europe and America because of their choice to marry an African man. The group dealt with all kinds of challenges that foreign wives faced including adapting to the culture and country and finding employment. It also helped women who found themselves in abusive marriages by providing shelter and raising money for them to start new lives.

Today Nigerwives-Nigeria is still growing strong with branches all over Nigeria supporting foreign wives.

House boy/girl: In British colonial times in Africa and Asia it was common for the British to have a person working in their house as a cook and cleaner. The house boy/girl would wear a uniform and as well as cooking and cleaning they would stand at attention at the dining room table and serve their masters meals. The job was sought after because the British paid a good salary and provided accommodation for the employee and their family in the form of boys' quarters within the compound of the home. Some also paid for the education of their house boy's/ girl's children.

The term was adopted by Nigerians and the practice carried on through Independence and up to today with many Nigerians employing domestic workers. Although it is offensive to call a grown man or woman a 'boy' or 'girl', the word was used during the time setting of the novel so I chose to use it.

PART I

PART I

CHAPTER 1

My childhood was relatively happy up until The Incident – the first time I understood my father was not well. The Incident is the dividing mark in my life: Before and After.

Before, things were simpler. Not perfect – looking back, I was aware that there was something going on beneath the surface of our happy family life – but it was kept behind closed doors, didn't have a name, and either I didn't see or didn't want to.

It's coming up to the five-year memorial next month and we are all going back to Nigeria. It's making me think about things, my life, my family, what we could have been, what we lost.

Lagos, 1982

We live in Ikoyi, a pleasant neighbourhood in Lagos. Our house is a bungalow with five bedrooms and huge gardens. There's me, my parents, and my older siblings, Sophie, Luke and Maggie.

I've always been the odd one out, probably because of the large age difference between us. I'm eight years old. Sophie is twenty-one, Luke is seventeen and Maggie is fifteen. My mother likes to call me her miracle baby. She named me Lily because I reminded her of a canna lily, her favourite flower. I guess it's nice, but it marked me as different from the start.

Maggie is the prettiest. She's like a princess with her soft hair curled into perfect little ringlets. It's so annoying. I don't understand how she has *that* and I have the frizz that stands up on my head like a sweeping brush. It doesn't seem fair.

The priest comes to visit my mum every week. I think they are friends because they are both Irish and miss their home. Mum gets out the best china teacups and they talk about rolling green fields and the smell of cow dung. Once when Father Burke was at our house, Maggie walked past and he looked up at her in a strange way and said, 'That Maggie, she's a looker. You better be careful. She'll attract the boys like bees to honey and land herself in a whole lot of trouble.' He wagged his finger at my mum as he said this and I could tell Mum was angry because her face went red as she spoke in a low flat voice.

'Watch the way you talk about my daughter.'

My oldest sister Sophie is also very pretty but in a different way from Maggie. Sophie wears her frizzy hair in a big Afro and she has this cool style, all large gold hoop earrings, flared jeans and platform shoes.

Sophie's always irritated and ignores me most of the time. Sometimes I do things just to annoy her, so she has no choice but to pay attention to me. When her friends from university come over, they *love* to talk to me. They say I am cute and look at me as though they would like to take me home. It drives Sophie mad. I think it makes her like me even less.

My brother Luke is the nicest. When I had the measles, the rash went up right inside me. It hurt so much for me to pee that I cried every time. Mum had to work so Luke stayed home from school to look after me. He read me my favourite stories and brought me all my meals in bed. He even made a chocolate cake. He's talented like that – he can do anything. He's always playing with a Rubik's Cube. I love to listen to him solve it over and over again, the soothing sound of *crick-crick-crick* as he twists the square.

Luke loves animals. He has a huge fish tank which he keeps in the lounge. It's like watching TV. There are so many different types of fish in there. I like the angelfish best. Their skin is white and shiny and they float around in pairs. If I trace my finger along the smooth glass, the fish will follow, back and forth.

Whenever we are all at home and in the same room, the atmosphere gets tense. It's like my siblings know something bad is about to happen and won't tell me what it is. I just know it has to do with my father.

In those moments, the one thing that can make them all relax is remembering their childhood together, before I was born, when they lived in the big house in the railway compound and Dad was a hospital supervisor and they went on lots of holidays abroad.

Mum says, 'Do you remember when we had tea in the Dorchester?' and my siblings nod and close their eyes as though they are back there. Then someone says, 'What about all those trips to Switzerland? Do you remember that creepy hotel in Vevey?' Everyone laughs and adds their own memories.

Once, I asked Luke what it was like on the railway compound. He smiled, showing me all his teeth, and said it was a magical place built on the old Botanical Gardens with plants and forests all around. Our house was the biggest, right next to the swamp.

'There were mammy waters living in there,' he said.

'What are they?'

'They're mermaids. They sit on the banks of the swamp at night among the reeds and sing.'

I listen to these stories and find it hard to imagine so much harmony in my family. It's as though they are describing different people.

CHAPTER 2

Manchester, 1990

There always seemed to be a barrier between me and my parents when I was young. My mother was always so busy and tired, working or recovering from work or looking after my father, apparently in a constant state of harassment or irritation. I wished and wished that she would just come and sit and talk with me for a while; but she didn't, so I had to find my own ways to comfort myself. I knew my mother loved me and that she felt guilty that she couldn't give me more of her attention – maybe this made the pain even harder. My father was a different story, a strange presence in my life. He rarely engaged with me or my siblings, mostly silent and unhearing. Somehow even when we were in the same room, he was always far away, elsewhere, impossible to reach.

Lagos, 1982

Mum works in a company that builds houses. She helps the boss. I think her job is very important because sometimes she has to work late and she always looks tired when she gets home. As soon as she comes in the door, she heads to the freezer, plops some ice cubes into a glass and then walks to the drinks cabinet and takes out the bottle of Martini. She pours until the glass is almost full and then closes her eyes and sips, mellowing. When the glass is empty, she goes to bed for her afternoon nap.

Mum often gets headaches and takes two round white tablets. In the mornings her eyes look small in her face and her lips look bigger than usual.

When I have Mum's full attention, I feel a kind of wild joy. I want to climb into that feeling and stay there. Sometimes, when I have a bad dream, Mum and Dad let me sleep in their bed between them. I like to press up against Mum, while she wraps an arm around me, and we become one person. It's the safest place I know.

Sometimes I wish I could rewind time. I'd go back to when I was four and I hadn't started school and Mum stayed home with me all day. Each morning we worked in the garden. She would wear her wide-brimmed straw hat with the blue ribbon, and on her hands a pair of bright yellow gloves. She had a special spade and a metal watering can. I had a toy spade, fork and bucket. We spent hours, kneeling on the ground, digging, planting, patting down soil with our fingers. As the sun grew higher in the sky, Mum would wipe her forehead and sigh.

'This heat,' she would say. 'Time to go in, Lily.'

At lunch, Dad would come home from his clinic. While we ate he would complain about his day, the patients pretending to be poorly. I liked it best when it was just Mum, me and the world of the garden.

I don't think Dad likes me very much. He rarely speaks to me. Sometimes he looks straight through me. Once, he leaned towards me and said in a low voice, 'Your mother is a cow.' My insides twisted up in knots.

Everyone is careful around Dad.

He shouts when Luke comes back late, or hangs out with *the wrong crowd*, or isn't studying enough. Dad also shouts at Sophie because he doesn't like her boyfriend. I think that's why she stays at the university dorms in Ibadan most of the time. When we're all out together as a family, that dark feeling settles over us. Mum whispers, 'Don't upset your father,' and we all know what she means. She won't relax until she has a couple of Martinis.

Sometimes he sits by himself in the lounge for hours just staring into space. When he does this, I picture him as a sleeping dragon – you have to hold your breath and creep past quietly in case he wakes up.

Dad reminds me of one of Luke's Rubik's Cubes – impossible for me to solve. One minute he's cold and silent, the next he's pacing back and forth like an animal trapped in a cage, talking loudly to himself and patting his pockets like he is searching for a weapon. His eyes flash and he shakes his head as though he's having an argument with someone. When he gets like this, we all clear out of the way and wait until the slap of his slippers on the terrazzo floor stops, and then Mum goes to find him. Often, after that, he goes to bed and sleeps for several days. After one of his long sleeps, he comes out of their bedroom, scratches his chin, looks around and laughs at nothing at all. I know it's not happy laughter because his eyes grow wide and frightened. When he does this, I feel frightened.

*

It's September and I am back at school. We had to write an article about what we did during the summer holidays. I wrote about our trip to California – the first time I've ever been away with the whole family. We went to Sea World and a huge killer whale jumped out of the water and splashed us. We went for a long walk in a forest of enormous trees called redwoods, taller than any I've ever seen before. It was very peaceful, the wind made a singing noise as it moved through the branches and even Dad was happy.

Seeing my parents in a new place made me notice different things about them. Like, when we were at the airport my father walked ahead of us, hands behind his back, while my mother and siblings struggled to push all our luggage trolleys. I wondered why Mum didn't ask him to help, but instead bit into her lip and tried to contain her fury.

It's horrible when they are angry with each other. It usually starts with my dad complaining, 'Why did you do that?' My mum snaps back, then they both grow quiet – it's this part that I hate because, when they are silent, the room becomes smaller and I know Mum is trying not to cry. But sometimes, Dad surprises everyone – in California, he made her breakfast in bed and I have never seen Mum as delighted as she was that morning.

On that holiday I met my grandmother. She is a beautiful woman with blonde hair and bright blue eyes. She has a thin face with a small mouth. She wears fancy clothes and has a giant black poodle called Monty who wears a red bow on his head. Every time I tried to pat him, he growled. I think Monty is very spoilt because the TV was always tuned to *his* favourite programme and when I changed it he barked and ran to my grandmother as though he were telling on me. Monty always got his way.

The first time I saw my grandmother she stared and didn't smile. She asked me some questions in a strange accent that I found difficult to understand. She told me I had to always call her Auntie Mary, never Nana or Grandma.

One time we went shopping in a store called Macy's and the assistant at the counter asked my mother and my grandma if they were sisters. My mother laughed and corrected her mistake but when they'd finished paying, my grandma said in a low furious voice, 'Don't you *ever* do that again.' My mum shrunk in on herself. I had a funny feeling in my chest when I saw this, as though my heart was a wet rag. 'Auntie Mary' didn't speak to my mother for the rest of the day. Later, back at home, Dad asked how our day was. Mum pushed past him into their bedroom and banged the door shut. My father looked at the door, shook his head and pursed his lips. 'That woman,' he said quietly. For once, I don't think he was talking about my mother. I didn't write all this in my school article.

Life at home can be lonely. I often wish I had a twin sister. I know that twins are bad luck, but I don't care. Our house boy, Sunday, told me his family left him and his twin brother on the steps of the missionary church when they were just a week old. He said he was lucky they weren't killed at birth as was the custom in his village. When Sunday told me this, I was sad for him and his brother and thought back to all the times when I had stepped on purpose in the dirt he had just swept up, or when I jumped on the sofa and threw the cushions on the floor while he tried to tidy up. I'm not often naughty, especially with my parents, but sometimes when the air at home seems so full of tension that I have to hold my breath, I lash out – and Sunday is an easy target.

After school, I play with our driver's two daughters – Hope and Happiness. They live in a small building in our compound. We play ten-ten, pat-a-cake, tag, and hide and seek in the garden. They call me *oyinbo*, but they don't say it in a bad way like some people do. The younger one, Happiness, likes to touch my paler skin and say, 'Fine oyinbo girl.' She always smiles when she says this.

Hope and Happiness are wary when we play together. If I fall or hurt myself, which I often do because I am very clumsy, they say *sorry* a hundred times even though it's not their fault, and make me go inside where it is safer.

The girls speak Igbo and a little pidgin English. Dad speaks

Igbo to their father, Peace, and to his friends when they visit. He looks more relaxed when he speaks in his own language so I thought it would impress him if I learnt Igbo. Yesterday I asked Hope to teach me how to say, 'Good afternoon, Father'. *Ehihie Ọma, nna.* I repeated the words and Hope tried her best not to laugh at my wobbly pronunciation. I made her say it again and again. We practised until she nodded and said I was ready. Then I went inside to find my father. He was sitting in his usual armchair, reading the newspaper.

I stood in front of him, cleared my throat and said, '*Ehihie Ọma, nna.*'

I thought I saw a look of pride flitter across his face like a moth, but then he darkened and snapped at me.

'Where did you learn that?'

'From Hope.'

'Have I not told you to stop playing with Peace's children?' Hissing through his teeth, he leaned forward and shook his head. 'This is your mother's fault – where is she that she is allowing you to run wild? That woman.'

He shook his paper up in front of his face, putting an end to the matter. Ashamed, confused and upset, I ran to my room, got under the covers and held my blankie under my nose.

Sometimes my dad does like me. Whenever we play football together in the garden, he laughs a lot and his eyes shine like stars. And when he came back from his last trip to London, he brought me a Sindy doll. She is beautiful and looks like Mum and I love brushing her long dark hair and changing her outfits. Dad even got me a Sindy car; it's yellow and looks like our jeep.

13

Once a week after school Dad takes me to the Rec Club for lunch. None of the others are invited, so I feel very special. All the people at the club greet him, 'Good afternoon, Dr Ekezie', like he is someone important.

I always have fish and chips and Dad has egusi stew with rice. After lunch we move to the verandah which looks out over the playground and Dad gives me fifty kobo for a donkey ride. The donkey man wears a small round hat, a long blue dress and baggy blue trousers. His skin is so black it's almost blue and he has tribal slashes on his cheeks. He helps me up onto the animal's back and leads it around the playground. I want Dad to see that I'm not afraid, but he's never watching.

There aren't usually any other children there because it's the hottest time of the day and most of the European children have gone for their siesta, so when I get bored of playing on my own or the sun starts to burn my skin, I go to find Dad and his friends and sit quietly and wait until he notices me. Watching Dad with his friends, it's as though someone has switched a light on in a dark room. He smiles, laughs, waves his hands about, sometimes he slaps his knee and lets out a belly laugh. His voice sounds out like the boom of waves against the shore.

It's not like that when the expatriates are there. Then, his voice lowers and he holds his hands on his lap or one around a bottle of beer while the other rests on the table. His body is tense, everything tightly coiled. If someone makes a joke, he smiles politely and gives a little half chuckle. It reminds me of how I was on my first day of school. When I see my father like that, I want to hug him to make him feel better.

It's often when the expatriates are there, though, that he

finally notices me. 'Ah, there you are. This is my daughter Lily.' They look at me and smile and nod and the women sometimes pat me on the head and say things like 'What a cute little girl' or 'Oh she's *very* fair, isn't she?' and Dad beams and says, 'My wife is Irish.' And everyone nods as though he's a pupil at school and they are all teachers.

CHAPTER 3

Manchester, 1990

School was always difficult for me. I struggled to fit in. Back in Lagos, I went to the British school, which was mainly for expatriates who were often just passing through. There were some Nigerians, a few Indians and one or two half-castes like me. I always had a sense of being trapped when I was there. As soon as I passed through the gates my chest would tighten. I think it had something to do with all the rules and the feeling of being under the teachers' control.

I often daydreamed in class. I could transport myself anywhere in my mind, it was my way of escape, of soothing my nerves. I was so good at it that sometimes I was slow to follow instructions or I didn't respond when a teacher asked me a question. This was when I got shouted at, and when that happened it was like someone waking me up with a freezing cold bucket of water. One teacher used to make me stand in the corner of the room, facing the wall. As I stood there with my head down I had a sick feeling in my belly because everyone's eyes were on my back, all of them thinking I was bad and stupid.

Lagos, 1983

We are a few weeks into the new school year and I'm still getting used to all the new faces in my class. I'm not very good with groups, I'm too quiet and get left out or pushed to the side. I like having one friend at a time, but I'm always scared they will make friends with someone more interesting and dump me. I think this is what happened with my siblings.

Last year there was a Strawberry Shortcake doll craze at school. All the English girls had these funny little dolls with red hair and freckles on their pale skin. I didn't understand what was so special about them until one girl held a doll right up to my nose and told me to smell it. I inhaled the sweetness of strawberries and sugar and got so excited I licked the doll's face. The English girls all shrieked and shouted 'EEEW!' as if I'd actually licked one of them and not just a piece of plastic, then they all started laughing at me.

I'm in the principal's office because the teachers all hate me. This time it's Mrs Stewart, but she's not the only one.

It started with Mrs Fernandez. She's a Nigerwife, like Mum.

I was in her class two years ago and she made my life a living hell. She shouted at me, pointing her ruler and calling me a 'lazy, stupid girl!' It was always me she picked on, never anyone else. I don't think it was because I am half-caste, because there was another half-caste girl in my class, Wando, and she didn't ever get it in the neck like I did. One of the problems I had with Mrs Fernandez's class was that I just couldn't see the blackboard. From where I sat, near the back, it was like trying to see into the bottom of a muddy pond, all the words merged into one murky gloop. As a consequence, I was always messing up and falling behind.

If she had been more sympathetic, she would have realized I was struggling with my eyesight. I don't know why I didn't just tell her what the problem was, but something inside me clammed up whenever she was around. She would stare at me with such frustration and fury, and I couldn't understand what it was about me that made her so mad. Then I thought about how my siblings ignored me or laughed at me at home, how my father overlooked me. Perhaps Mrs Fernandez simply understood what they already knew – that I was no good. They just didn't want me there.

Mrs Fernandez turned me into a coward. Even after another teacher finally put two and two together, and Mum and Dad took me to get my glasses, she still found reasons to shout at me. One day, I was too slow coming to the board to write a word and she went berserk. At one point I thought she was going to hit me. She screamed and shouted, called me all kinds of names. I held the tears back for as long as I could, but they just kept on dribbling down my face. The whole class was staring. There was something wrong with me and Mrs Fernandez knew it.

That lunchtime I went and sat alone in a corner of the playground. One of the assistants, Mrs Obi, saw me and came over. She sat on the bench beside me and put her arm around my shoulder. She was young and had a kind face.

'Why are you crying, child? Ah ah! What has happened to you? Ehh?'

I could see she cared and was trying to help, so I wanted to say *something*, but I couldn't tell her about Mrs Fernandez in case I got into even more trouble. So I pointed at two black boys who were kicking a ball to each other in the playground nearby.

'*They* hurt me.'

I will never forget the look on those boys' faces as Mrs Obi grabbed each by the ear, scolded them and led them away for a punishment. For weeks afterwards, I couldn't sleep at night and I lost my appetite. When Mum asked what was wrong, I couldn't tell her.

I think that's when I realized that I was not the only victim of my cowardice. My fear made me feel so vulnerable that I would rather hurt others than stand up to the real bully. I promised myself that the next time a teacher picked on me – and I knew there would soon be a next time – I would find it in myself to be a little bit braver. So that's why, when I stood in the doorway of Mrs Stewart's classroom this morning, listening to her shout at me yet again for being late, something shifted. I felt heat rise from my belly up to my head, and I turned and ran to see the principal.

The principal's office is cool with air conditioning and I sit in a leather chair opposite her large wooden desk and start to simmer down and gather my thoughts. Mrs Stewart never asks me *why* I'm late, or if she does, she doesn't want to hear the answer. I'm late for the same reason I'm always late – because in the mornings Daddy is groggy from the tablets he takes every night and so he doesn't always get up in time to get me to school, and Mum can't do it because she has to leave for work so early.

The principal is new, she's a Nigerwife and always wears traditional clothes and even speaks Yoruba. She's the kind of Nigerwife my mother disapproves of, the kind who 'go native' as she calls it, because that means they are turning their backs on their own culture and Mum says women should never give up who they are just to please a man.

The principal smiles at me.

'How can I help you, Lily?'

'It's Mrs Stewart. She keeps on shouting at me and she never shouts at anyone else. It isn't fair. Today she shouted at me for being late but it isn't my fault. My daddy can't get up in the morning because of his special tablets so sometimes I'm late when he brings me.'

The smile drops from her face and her eyebrows move together.

'I'm sorry to hear that, Lily. Look, shall we call Mrs Stewart in and have a chat with her all together?' Her voice is gentle.

I nod and listen. She calls her secretary and tells her to bring Mrs Stewart to her office. A tingle of pleasure runs through me.

Mrs Stewart looks different standing here. Smaller and less intimidating. The principal gestures at a wicker chair next to mine and Mrs Stewart drops heavily into it.

'Lily tells me you have been having some problems.'

Mrs Stewart's face turns red and she bites on her bottom lip. 'She doesn't pay attention in class and is constantly late.'

'Well, the lateness is not Lily's fault and I will speak to her parents about that to see if some other arrangement can be made for her to get to school on time. You live in Ikoyi, yes, Lily? Perhaps one of the other parents nearby will give you a lift.'

Mrs Stewart doesn't say anything.

'Right. Now, Lily, I know you have a tendency to daydream in class. I would like you to try harder to pay attention to your lessons.'

She then looks at Mrs Stewart.

'Mrs Stewart, maybe if you try to engage Lily more in class rather than just punishing her you will get better results. What do you think?'

Mrs Stewart seems lost for words. She nods her head.

'All right then, that's resolved.'

As I walk back to class with Mrs Stewart I keep expecting her to turn and slap me or something, but the revenge never comes. She walks ahead in silence and for the rest of the day she leaves me alone. I feel as if I am breathing freely for the first time.

CHAPTER 4

Manchester, 1990

In the period when Maggie and Luke had gone to boarding school in England and Sophie was miles way at the University of Ibadan, it felt like there was a vacuum at home that I couldn't fill. The house was so very quiet without them. I was used to being alone even when surrounded by people but it was the effect that their absence caused on my parents that made me lonely. My mother drank more and she often stared at the phone as though willing it to ring but it never did. She went to check our PO Box every day and when she discovered a letter she would place it carefully into her handbag and hold it on her lap until we got home and then she would race into her room and close the door. She would come out later with a fresh glow on her face and a smile playing on her lips.

When my siblings left, my father became even more withdrawn. Sitting for hours on the verandah, staring at the garden but not really seeing it. Or he would disappear for long walks on Bar Beach. This would upset my mother because she was afraid he might be attacked by armed robbers and they would often have fights about it when he came home. My father's interactions with me became even more limited; he stopped taking me to the Rec Club with him or dropping me at school. I felt that he hated me for being the one left behind.

Lagos, 1983

It's the week before Christmas. Maggie and Luke are coming home from boarding school for the holidays. Sophie will be here too. Mum and Dad are really excited. Dad is sitting at the dining room table planning family activities in his diary and I'm helping Mum decorate the huge artificial Christmas tree in the lounge. I hang red, silver and gold baubles on the branches and watch as Mum climbs up on a chair to put the silver angel on top. It's covered with silver glitter that comes off onto your skin when you touch it. When she finishes, she looks down at me and smiles. Her face sparkles.

*

Luke's in a wheelchair. We all went to the airport to get him and Mum made a small gasping noise when she saw a half-caste girl push him out into the arrivals hall with a pair of crutches across his knees and one leg in a thick plaster cast.

23

'What happened?' Mum and Dad ask at the same time.

Luke looks down at his leg and shrugs his shoulders. 'I broke it sledging. The school said they sent you a letter.'

'You careless boy! Why didn't you tell us? Have you been treated properly? How did you manage to travel?' Dad's voice is loud and people are staring.

'Ijeoma helped me,' Luke replies.

The girl behind Luke smiles. Her hair is braided with small beads attached to the ends, which make a clicking sound as she moves. Her parents step forward and the mother smiles at Mum. I think they know each other. All the Nigerwives do.

'It was no problem, we found him in Departures at Heathrow. The school had just dumped him there with all his luggage.' She shook her head.

'So grateful to you. Thank you so much.' Dad cups her hand in both of his and then does the same with the father. Once they are gone, Dad puts his hands on his hips and studies Luke's leg.

'They shouldn't have put you on a plane. Look how swollen your toes are. You stupid boy! What foolish nonsense were you doing that you broke your leg? Ehh?' He looks at Luke in disgust and marches off without us.

Luke unzips the bag resting on his knees, pulls out a ruler, slides it under the cast and scratches, closing his eyes in relief.

'Sorry oh,' I say and place my hand on his shoulder. He gives me a wobbly smile.

I point at his graffitied cast. 'Can I write on it, too?'

'Sure.'

Mum hugs Luke.

'Did they at least give you something for the pain? Do you

want some Veganin?' She rustles around in her large leather handbag and pulls out a foil pill packet that only has two tablets left. She stares at them with a worried expression before pressing the tablets out and handing them to Luke. 'We'll have to stop at the pharmacy to get some more on the way home. Don't mind your daddy, he's just worried about you.'

'He has a strange way of showing it,' says Luke. 'I hate him.'

Luke's bottom lip shakes and there are tears in his eyes. I look away because it hurts to see him like that. My brother, 'The Pup' as Mum still calls him. Mum pats Luke on the shoulder and says, 'Let's get you home.' She calls a porter to help with the suitcases and then pushes Luke towards the exit.

Dad is waiting in the car, sitting in the back. The passenger seat in the front has been pushed all the way back. Peace jumps out and heaves the suitcases into the boot. He helps Luke out of his chair. Luke hops on his one good leg into the front seat. When he is settled, Peace puts a hand on the cast, closes his eyes and says, 'I go pray for you, my pikin. This thing will heal in Jesus' Almighty Name.'

I'm sitting between Mum and Dad; his breathing is heavy and noisy next to me. Throughout the journey, he doesn't speak. He leans his elbow on the car door and places his thumb against his mouth as though trying to stop words coming out.

Mum tries to fill the silence, asking Luke about school. Luke gives one-word answers and stares out the window. I hold onto my Sindy doll and try to distract myself with a game but the air in the car makes me afraid.

*

25

A few days later Maggie and Sophie come home. All of us are together. The house is so different. Full of voices and laughter. Mum spends hours listening to each of them give her updates about their lives. Mum loves this; there's a light in her eyes and she concentrates hard as she listens to each of their stories. I linger behind partially open doors, listening and watching. She always talks to them separately, and after they have finished telling her what's been happening to them, she leans forward and says, 'I've missed you so much. You know you're my favourite, pet.'

Now Mum and Dad are having their afternoon nap, so we all sit in the lounge and they talk about their adventures. I crouch on the floor with my notebook so I don't miss anything important. It feels so good for the house to be alive with their laughter and voices.

Luke tells us how he broke his leg sledging down a hill on a plastic bag with a group of other boys. He makes a cracking noise to show how it broke and how painful it was.

'I bet Dad told you off,' says Sophie. She spreads out her fingers and looks at her nails as she says this. They are painted bright red and have a pretty shape.

Luke clicks his fingers and whistles. 'I thought he was going to beat me when he saw the cast.'

Sophie shakes her head. 'That's our father now. If you break a leg, he wants to break the other to teach you a lesson!'

They all laugh, strong belly laughs that make them slap their thighs and clap their hands. I don't see what is so funny. I notice my siblings always make jokes about our father's strictness. They like to share stories, each claiming to be punished the worst. It's as though they are sharing something painful, but laughing about it takes the sting away.

Luke looks over at me. 'Hey, Lily, come here and write on my cast.'

I kneel by his side and use a black crayon to draw a man. Dad. Then I add Mum, Sophie, Luke, Maggie, in order of their ages. I lean back and look at my work and realize there isn't any white space left. I hesitate for a moment, before adding myself next to Maggie.

Luke smiles strangely and stares at the family on his leg.

'I discovered in England that I'm black.'

I return to my notebook and write *Black*.

'You know how people love half-castes here? It's different over there. One weekend, a group of us went to the village and someone called the police!'

'Say what?' Sophie slaps her knee.

I draw a sad face in my notebook.

'There were four of us. Me, you know that boy Ayo from St Gregs, Matthew, and Emeka. When we went into the shops, the people stared at us as though we were feral. Especially white women. I think they thought we were going to jump on them.' He lifts one side of his mouth into a half-smile. 'Anyway, before long a police car turns up. Two policemen get out and ask us what we are doing. I explained we were from the boarding school and just doing some shopping. When they realized we were from that school, their attitude changed completely. They probably thought we were the sons of presidents.'

Sophie sucks air through her teeth and makes a hissing

sound. 'But what about the school? What are the English kids like to you?'

Luke studies his leg before replying. 'Well, to be honest, I spend my free time with the Africans and halfs. Some of the English boys are bastards. Real ignorant, you know. Talking to me about jungles and huts and wild animals. And asking me if I want a banana.' This sends a wave of laughter around the room.

Sophie shakes her head. 'When Daddy sent me to a boarding school in England it was terrible. I was the only black person in the whole school. Can you imagine?' Her eyes grew wide. 'Ah ah, those girls were the nastiest, most ignorant group of people I ever came across. When I used to go into their stuffy common room, they would start sniffing the air with those turned-up piggy noses of theirs.' Sophie uses her finger to pull up the tip of her nose and sniffs. *'There's a bad smell in here. We better open the windows.'*

Luke winces as he scratches under his cast with the ruler. 'Shebi you suffered oh, Sophie!'

Maggie lays her palm on Sophie's shoulder. 'That's awful.'

'I didn't put up with it for long. Ha! Me?' Sophie points at her chest. 'I ran away in the middle of the night. Hitched a ride with a lorry driver to London. I called my friend Josephine and she came to collect me.'

'What happened when you got home?' asks Maggie.

'I thought Daddy would kill me.' She flicks her hand quickly so her fingers make a snapping noise. 'He sat me down and made to unbuckle his belt while he gave me a lecture. First, he asked me why I would do such a thing to this family. To disgrace us in such a dishonourable manner. You know how he likes his high-sounding English when he's angry with us.'

Sophie makes her voice deep as she imitates our father. 'I send you to the most expensive boarding school in Great Britain, the school of *royalty* no less, and you complain they are racist!'

'Oh lord!' Maggie rolls her eyes.

'Then he went on to tell me that I was too too spoilt and life had been too too easy for me and I needed to suffer more to understand life better. Blah Blah Blah. In the end, he didn't beat me and he didn't send me back.'

Luke grips the ruler so tightly that his knuckles turn yellow.

Sophie shakes her head as though to remove those bad memories from her mind and turns to Maggie. 'What about you, princess?'

'I haven't had any problems, but I stick with my own kind and the white girls stick together.'

I draw a picture of Maggie in my notebook, paying close attention to getting the spirals of her hair correct.

'I love it in England,' says Maggie. 'It's so much better than being in this backward country.'

'You are such a silly girl!' Sophie spits the words and Maggie flinches and bites her bottom lip. Sophie sucks her teeth.

*

It's Christmas Eve and I can't concentrate during midnight mass, I'm too excited. As we leave church, I tell Maggie my plan. 'I'm going to try and catch Santy tonight.'

She narrows her eyes and whispers in my ear, 'There is no Santa Claus.'

'You're lying! And he's Santy not Santa!'

'Quiet!' says Dad as we pile into the car and I glare at Maggie with all the hate in my being.

At bedtime, I carry my blanket and pillow to the lounge and settle myself on the sofa with the lights on and a book. But Mum finds me.

'What are you doing?'

'Waiting for Santy.'

'You can't. You'll frighten him away. Come on now, get to bed.' She takes my hand and leads me towards the hall door.

I pull back. 'Maggie said Santy isn't real.'

Mum gasps. 'What? That little brat! Who does she think she is telling you that?'

Off she strides and before long I hear her shouting at Maggie. I run to her bedroom and peek in. Maggie is in bed with her knees pulled into her chest.

'How dare you? How dare you tell her there's no Santy! Who gave you the right?'

'I didn't mean to. I'm sorry, Mummy.' Tears form in her eyes.

'Selfish girl.' Mum turns and leaves. I run and hide behind the hallway door and, when I'm sure the coast's clear, I creep back to the bedroom and peer in. Maggie is sniffing and sobbing but I don't feel sorry for her. Instead, I have a kind of hungry joy because Maggie *never* gets into trouble. It's always Luke or Sophie, or me, who gets told off. Sophie even told me I was lucky because when she and Luke were my age, they used to get beatings. Mum said she used to beat Luke to protect

30

him from Dad because if it were Dad, he might have killed him. But Maggie was never beaten and is rarely even shouted at. I think it's because Maggie is so beautiful. That's why our parents treat her special, like a princess. And this makes me realize that beauty is more than just looking good. It's better. Beauty can protect you.

Maggie buries her head under the blanket and I go back to my room, climb into my bed and try to stay awake so that I will hear Santy.

*

The presents are under the tree and each has a name label on it. I race to find mine and tear them open. This is the happiest I've been all year. I don't know where to start, whether to play with my new Sindy horse or open the box full of books called *The Chronicles of Narnia*. I watch as my mother carefully unwraps her gift from Dad. It's a black velvet box. She opens it and inside is a gold necklace, bracelet and earrings.

He takes the necklace and holds it up. There are small masks dangling from the chain. 'These masks are copied from a famous Benin carving of a king.'

'Oh, how beautiful!'

Dad helps Mum put the necklace and bracelet on and she hurries to the mirror in the hall.

'Thank you,' she says. They smile at each other, and in that moment the room is full of love.

CHAPTER 5

Manchester, 1990

When I was little I resented my siblings for taking up space in my family and then disappearing one after the other and leaving an emptiness behind that I couldn't fill. I tried so hard to be one of them – they all shared something that only people who have grown up together can have, like they could speak their own unique language. They knew things that I didn't and when I made my childish attempts to join in their conversations about our parents or about how unpredictable life was in our country or about anything that I thought might interest them they laughed at me, or my brother would tousle my head. This angered me greatly and I would often run off to a corner of the garden and simmer silently, wishing they would all die terrible deaths.

Lagos, 1983

It's New Year's Eve and we are at Bar Beach. I love digging holes in the sand, to see if I can reach the centre of the Earth, but after a while I get bored and walk towards the sea.

'Stop right there!' I'm pulled roughly back. 'How many times have I told you not to go near the water! You bold, bold girl!' yells Mum.

Every child here knows the Atlantic Ocean is dangerous. Its currents are so strong they can snatch you away and drown you in a heartbeat.

I sit down and sulk in the sand.

'Don't you make that face at me, it will get stuck like that in the wind. You just wait until we get back ... Jesus, Mary and Joseph, what is he doing?' I look up and see Mum staring far out at the water with a look of alarm. It's Dad, swimming amid waves as tall as houses.

'He's going to get himself killed!'

We go through this drama every time. I don't understand what all the fuss is about – he hardly even appears out of breath after a swim, let alone at risk of drowning.

When Dad comes back, we pack up and walk to the car. Me, Luke and Maggie pile in together. Sophie has gone back north to university. As we drive off from the beach, it's immediately clear that something's not right. There are no people out on the street and only a few cars on the road. Which is odd for Lagos. Suddenly, an army jeep full of soldiers drives up behind us and a tremendous noise makes me clamp my hands over my ears. The soldiers are all up on their feet, waving guns and shooting rounds into the air. The jeep gets nearer and one of the soldiers stares into our car. His eyes meet mine. He is about the same age as Luke, holding a machine gun. He smiles at me and waves.

One of the other soldiers shouts something at us and then they speed past. In the back of the jeep I see three men. Their clothes are bloody and torn and their hands are tied behind their backs with rope. I've never seen people look so scared.

'Oh god!' says Mum. I can't see her face but I can tell she is frightened; her back is as straight as a ruler and she keeps running her fingers through her hair. Dad breathes heavily; he is driving because Peace is on holiday. His hands grip the steering wheel tightly as he speeds ahead. Maggie's body tenses next to mine. She sucks her thumb. She only does that when she's upset.

When we get home, Mum rushes to phone the university but the line goes dead. We sit in the lounge and huddle together listening as gunshots pierce the silence like giant pins stabbing huge balloons in the sky. No one speaks. I notice Mum and Dad are holding hands, something they rarely do. When the phone rings, Mum pounces to answer. It's Sophie. She's safe in Ibadan. We all let out a big breath. Dad starts arguing with Luke about something. Maggie goes to her room. I go to my room to play with my Sindy doll.

Lagos, 1984

It's January and the house is quiet again. In the afternoons before Mum gets home, it's just me and Dad, which basically means it's just me because unless it's one of his good days, Dad mostly sleeps or sits in his chair staring into space.

I'm bored. TV doesn't start until 4 p.m. and the first fifteen minutes is the national anthem, so I end up in the garden. I wish I had someone to explore with. Tropical flowers and trees. All the colours of the rainbow. Mum taught me all their names. Orange canna lilies. Red hibiscus. Purple cordyline. Pink roses. Mother-in-law's tongue. There are banana trees at the back and a tall coconut tree at the front. Two parakeets live in one of the trees. They talk to each other constantly. Insects buzz and their multicoloured wings vibrate in the afternoon heat. I run my fingers over the leaves of the mimosa plant and they curl up as though frightened by my touch. An agama lizard comes out of a hibiscus bush. It has a black body with an orange head and tail. It nods as though greeting me then takes off back into the undergrowth.

A voice calls and I look up to see who it is. It's Daramola; he sometimes drives us around when Peace is busy with Mum. He sits in the back seat of the car eating a mango. He waves me over.

'Come here,' he says. He reaches across and opens the passenger door. I climb in; it is so natural to obey an elder even if he is the driver. He uses his knife to slice a piece of mango and he hands it to me. I take the mango but I don't want to eat it because he has touched it. I don't like it when people touch my food.

'Such a fine girl.'

I look up at him. There is something I don't like about him, I can't put it into words. It's more than his unpleasant appearance, the keloids on his cheeks where tribal marks have been slashed, his yellow teeth that are sharp like a wolf's and his eyes that are close together in his face. They travel over me like a torchlight.

'What a nice dress you wear.' It's my pink towelling dress that I always wear around the house. Something is on my leg. It's his hand – resting darkly against my skin. His nails are long and pointed like a woman's and they have dirt trapped under them. My heart hits against my ribs and my skin burns beneath his fingers. His hand slowly travels upwards. I squeeze my eyes shut. I want to move but can't.

'Lily, wetin oh nah do for that moto! Comot from that car and enter house, now, now.' It's the house boy Sunday. 'Comot!'

Suddenly, my body does what I tell it and I jump out of the car. Sunday pulls me back to the house by the arm and flashes Daramola such a glare that I am frightened. Sunday mutters under his breath in his own language as he closes the front door. He shakes his head and I can tell he is very angry from the way his face is all twisted.

Later that evening I am sitting in my bed staring out the window. My door opens and Mum comes in.

'Lily,' she says and comes and sits beside me on the bed. 'Sunday told me ... about Daramola.' Her eyes are large and expectant. 'Tell me what happened.'

'He asked me to get into the car and I did and ...' I move one shoulder up and my eyes go watery.

Mum grips my arms on both sides. 'Did he touch you?'

'Only my leg.'

She is so close to me her breath is on my skin. Her cheeks

are flushed and her voice wobbles. 'It's OK, Lily. I'll take care of this.'

She leans in and hugs me; she's holding me tighter than is comfortable but I don't mind because in her arms I know I am safe.

She gets up to leave and then turns and says, 'Don't mention any of this to your father. It would upset him too much. OK, Lily?' Her voice is hard so I nod but I have an urgent feeling inside me that I can't push down. What happened with Daramola was dangerous. What if it happens again?

Later when Mum is lying down for her afternoon siesta I go to where Daddy is sitting in the lounge. He is reading the newspaper. I stand in front of him and bite my lip, suddenly afraid.

'Daddy,' I say.

'What is it?'

'Daramola, he . . . he tried to touch me in the car,' I say.

Daddy puts his paper down and takes off his glasses. He leans forward and for the first time since my siblings left, his eyes are bright sparks in his head, completely focused on me.

'What do you mean?'

As I describe what happened my father's eyes grow large. I have the impression that he is an animal, getting ready to attack its prey. He jumps up from his seat and I get a shock. He rushes past me through the hall door into my parents' bedroom. I hear shouts and I run to see what's happening. Mum is sitting up in bed; she looks confused and frightened.

'Did you know about this?'

At first she shakes her head, eyes bleary and blurred from

sleep, but then she says, 'Yes, I've dealt with it. I fired him. We'll never see him again. I made sure of that.'

This doesn't make Daddy calm. He keeps pacing up and down and he balls his hands into fists. He is saying something in a low voice but I can't hear it. Mum jumps out of bed and goes to him.

'It's OK, Obi, calm down. She's all right.'

But her words aren't helping him; he starts touching the side of his head repeatedly as he walks to and fro. The gesture is light at first but then it becomes more forceful and he hits his temple with the heel of his hand over and over again. He is panting and sweat rolls down his face. I catch a glimpse of his eyes as he runs back and forth – they are wild, like two exploding stars in his face. My stomach tightens.

'Obi, come now, take this.' Mum is holding out a tablet to him. He bats her hand away and the tablet falls on the floor. Mum notices me standing in the doorway for the first time and her face drops.

'Lily, go to your room now!' she shouts.

I run to my room and get under the covers. What have I done? Mum told me not to tell Daddy and I did and now look at what's happened. I can hear their muffled voices from their room. I pull my cover over my head and listen to the sound of my breath. My heart is pounding so loudly it might jump out of my body. I stay like that until the voices go quiet. I wait in the silence and then I hear their door open and the gentle clack of Mum's slippers. She comes into my room.

'Lily, are you all right?'

'What's wrong with Daddy?'

She studies my wall. 'He's upset about what happened to you, that's all. I've given him some medicine to make him feel better. Don't worry, pet.' She rests her hand on mine and gives it a squeeze.

Later that evening I hear our gate being opened and the crunch of tyres on the gravel driveway. I get up and go to the lounge. A man gets out of a car; Mum is outside speaking to him. He is carrying a case just like Daddy's old doctor's case. He follows Mum into their bedroom and stays there for a long time. I go and listen at the door; they are all speaking with low voices and I can't make out what they are saying. I hear footsteps and run to my room. After the man leaves I go to Mum.

'What's happening?'

'That's Daddy's doctor, he's given him a special injection to make him feel better. Your daddy will need to rest for a few days so don't disturb him.'

I turn over this information in my mind. Daddy doesn't come down for dinner and the next day he still doesn't make an appearance.

'Is Daddy all right?' I ask Mum.

'Yes, he will be fine, he just needs to rest because he was very upset.'

I have made Daddy ill by telling him what happened. I shouldn't have said anything.

CHAPTER 6

Manchester, 1990

Once the effects of his medication wore off I sensed a new energy about my father. He often went out for meetings and came back in an excited mood. He would tell Mum all about the big plans he had and she would listen, her eyes narrowed. She told him not to get so excited, that there were risks and she didn't want him to be disappointed. She was careful with her words but I could tell she didn't approve. He would shake his head and bat his hand at her like he was waving away her negativity. I liked that he was in such a good mood. A few times during that period he came looking for me in the garden and called me to kick a ball with him, something he rarely did. He laughed as we kicked the ball back and forth and I was happier than I had ever been.

Lagos, 1984

January is harmattan season. The weather is cool and dry. There's a red haze in the air and lots of people have Apollo from the dust. We call it Apollo because the first Moon landing was called Apollo and on that day so many people got conjunctivitis that they thought alien dust from the Moon had come back to Earth and infected everyone.

I've managed to escape getting Apollo but my eyes feel gritty every time I am outside so I play inside most days.

A white man is sitting in the parlour with my parents. His name is Klausman. He has curly brown hair and a large moustache that twirls up at the ends. He is wearing a white short-sleeved shirt, khaki shorts and sandals with white socks pulled up over his ankles. I can see the dark hairs on his legs, like the rough hairs on a coconut shell. He has a huge stomach that curves like a ball and the buttons on his shirt fight to keep it covered. When he bends down to look at me, he grins and reveals two gold front teeth.

Dad tells me to go to my room but I hide in the hall, leaving the door ajar so I can still see them, and eavesdrop. *A factory. Great investment. Double your money in two years.* Dad is laughing but Mum is very serious. She keeps asking questions that make Klausman's face go red. When white people get angry or upset, they can't hide it. He turns to Dad.

'Do you let your wife do your business for you in this country?'

Dad turns to Mum. 'This is none of your concern.' His voice is like steel. 'I think you should leave us.'

I go to my room and wait for Mum to come and find me.

'What are you doing?'

'Nothing,' I say with a shrug. 'Who's that man?'

She leans against the doorframe, sighs, runs her hand through her hair and studies the ceiling.

'A man I don't trust, that's who.'

'He speaks strange.' I hold up Sindy and make a grown-up voice as I say this, as though she's talking.

'He's Austrian. That's a country in Europe.'

'What are they talking about?' Sindy asks.

'He says he'll make Daddy rich.'

'Will he?'

'I don't think so.'

Dad and Klausman say goodbye in the hallway. Dad shuts the front door and his leather slippers slap along the marble floor towards my bedroom. He arrives, grins and rubs his hands together like he has just won the lottery.

'Why the sour face?' he asks Mum, brightly.

'I told you I don't trust that man.'

'Ah. Enough. You are such a pessimist.' He moves his palm downwards at her which means shut up and walks away.

*

This afternoon after work Mum takes me to the Rec Club as a special treat. She's usually too tired, too busy, or has one of her headaches, so I can't believe my luck.

You can tell that it's an important place from the *wahalla* involved in getting into it every time we go there. The armed security guard reminds me of a cockerel I once saw strutting across the street. His features are sharp, like wood carvings.

The whites of his eyes are yellow and his face drips with sweat. A vein bulges on each temple.

He pesters the Nigerian children who come on their own with their parents' membership cards; acts as if they have no right to be there, getting angry and hurling insults before grudgingly letting them in. White people sail through. It isn't fair.

When Mum and I arrive, he's in full swing, shouting at a group of kids.

'You better comot for here before I go call am police!' he shouts. One of the boys pleads their case, waving his card. Members are allowed to bring two guests, but the boy has three friends with him. He turns to his friends and the other boys stare at him with large eyes. He presses his palms together and shakes his head from side to side.

'I beg, Sa, please a beg,' he says. 'My mother is inside, in the pool.'

He is about to cry. His friends are clutching their towels, bags, armbands, a large pink ring with a flamingo head.

'One of them can come in with me,' says Mum.

The guard eyes her nastily. She shows him her card.

He looks at me and hisses through his teeth. Mum often tells me Nigerwives are at the bottom of the pecking order in this country but he can't defy her. After all, her husband could be someone important.

He waves everyone through. There is much clapping and we all set off towards the chlorine smell of the swimming pool.

There are two large pools and a baby section. After we

43

change into our swimsuits, Mum directs me towards some sun loungers and we arrange our things.

Mum blows up my pink armbands and I hold up my arms for her to slip them on. She takes me by the hand to the shallow end of the big pool. There are loads of children in the water, splashing and screaming, and suddenly I get nervous. I slowly lower myself into the cool water.

Mum sits on the side kicking her feet in the water and she chats to one of the Nigerwives. I wade around hoping to find a friend, but I don't know anyone.

I see a girl with neat cornrows in her hair clinging to the side of the pool. I smile at her and she grins back. 'Can you do this?' she says.

She dives under the water and does a handstand. Her yellow soles poke up out of the surface. I try to copy her and realize that my armbands are preventing me. We laugh as I struggle against the water.

'Yinka! Give me the ball!' the girl shouts to someone. A large orange ball soars over and lands beside her.

'Let's play,' she says.

We throw the ball to each other and, for a while, I'm one of the happy people at the Rec Club swimming pool. I belong.

CHAPTER 7

Manchester, 1990

Dad's mood changed just a few days after his meeting with Mr Klausman. He no longer played with me or gave me any attention. He and Mum had heated discussions at the dining room table. They pored over documents with lots of numbers on them. Dad kept shaking his head and Mum bit her lower lip. At one point Dad held his head in his hands as though it might fall off his neck and then he started to cry. When I saw this happen something large and hard lodged in my throat and I couldn't swallow. I retreated to my bedroom and pulled the covers over myself. I knew that my world was about to change forever.

Lagos, 1984

It's exactly a week after that man Klausman visited my parents. The air is still dry and dusty from the harmattan winds. I've been stuck indoors all morning. In the afternoon the day is bright and hot and I set out to explore the garden. The ground is dry and cracked. I use my spade to dig a hole near the hibiscus bush. As I get deeper the soil softens, becomes rich and clumpy. All kinds of creatures crawl around, millipedes, beetles, ants. I spot an agama lizard nearby and squat down to its level. It nods its black head up and down at me and then scuttles away.

I run back to the house to get a drink and when I come through the front door – that's when time stops. They are in the hallway. Mum and a man. He is gripping her arm and she makes a muffled noise like an animal. He throws her to the ground. I turn and run to the boys' quarters, screaming for help. Peace comes running out and we race back to the house.

Mum is curled up on the floor. The man, I finally realize, is my father. He is kicking, making heavy grunting sounds. Neither of them says a word. This makes me more frightened.

Peace dives in. He pulls Dad away, pushes him back and pins him to the wall with his forearm. Mum is lying on her side; she uses a hand to push herself up to her knees. She has blood on the side of her head. I feel someone touch my shoulder; it's Blessing, Peace's wife. Peace shouts to her in Igbo. She runs to Mum, gathers her up and gently helps her onto the sofa. I go and sit beside her.

Sunday arrives with the gateman and they rush to help Peace with my father. They try to pin him tight against the

46

wall. Dad's face is like a mask. It's him but it's not him. He has found his voice now and is shouting. More people come inside the house.

I need to do something.

I grab the foghorn we use to scare away armed robbers and press it. At the same time a scream climbs out of my mouth.

For a moment, everyone is stunned into silence. Even Dad stops his raging.

With Blessing's help Mum limps to the phone in the hallway. She is holding her side. The men half carry, half drag Dad into the master bedroom and close the door. I sit back on the sofa. My lungs feel tight and I have to take small breaths.

Eventually Mum comes and finds me. As she sits down, I buckle into her. She gently rocks back and forth, one hand holding her left side. I put my arm around her but she doesn't respond or look at me.

*

A car horn beeps and I hear the scrape of the front gates being opened. I go to the window to see what's happening. Peace opens the door. There are three men standing there. Two of them are big and strong and all dressed in white. The third man is the same one who came that night when my father was upset about Daramola. He speaks to my mother – and, after a while, they go through to find my father in the bedroom. I dig my nails into my palms. I can hear the voices, raised, my father shouting. My mouth has dried up and I can't swallow and I can't find air to breathe. The sound of a slap, shoes slipping on marble and the thud of a body knocking a hard surface. Things are thrown.

The doctor comes out.

'Has his uncle arrived yet?' he asks my mother.

Mum shakes her head. 'They won't help me. What am I supposed to do?'

They continue talking but I'm not listening. I am very cold and start to shiver.

*

I hear my mother's voice coming from far away and there is a tight grip on my arm.

'Come on, Lily, we have to go.'

I notice it is dark outside.

*

Peace is driving us. No one says a word. I watch Peace in the rear-view mirror. He pulls out a handkerchief and wipes his nose and eyes. Mum stares at her hands and wrings them together over and over again and I know she's praying.

I focus on the houses as we pass them by. It's dark and the night sellers are out with their kerosene lamps. Women squat and cook akara balls or suya. The smell wafts through the window. They wrap the food in newspaper and hand them to hungry customers. We turn onto Awolowo road.

'Where are we going?' I ask.

'We are going to stay with Paul.'

We continue until we reach the lagoon and arrive at a large block of flats. We get out and then Mum tells Peace to go back and help look after Dad.

I like Paul. He is Irish and works with Mum and he always smiles at me. He says we can sleep in his spare bedroom. Mum has brought my blankie so I shut my eyes and hold it next to my cheek and smell it to make myself feel better. I put my forefinger in my mouth and suck. But I keep picturing Mum on the floor and Dad above kicking her. I am cold even though it's hot and my teeth start to chatter. I don't want to be alone with my thoughts in this strange room.

I wish Mum would come but she is talking to Paul in the lounge.

I push my nails into my arm until it bleeds. The sharpness is nice.

In the morning Mum's face has turned black on one side and her lower lip is swollen. I can't take my eyes off her as I sit at the breakfast table.

Paul has made pancakes with honey.

'Does it hurt?' I ask.

Mum shakes her head.

Paul asks me about school. I look up at him. He has such bright blue eyes. He asks about my favourite book, and I tell him it's *The Lion, the Witch and the Wardrobe*.

Mum is holding a cup of coffee, staring into space. It's like she's lost somewhere. Paul glances at her, and then back at me. His mouth is smiling but his eyes don't look happy.

I eat my pancakes silently. They are sweet and comforting.

'Shall we get you to school then?' He holds out his hand.

I nod and slip off my chair. Mum is still staring at something nobody else can see. She's gripping her cup like it's the edge of a cliff. This terrifies me.

*

Paul gave me a book, *Alice's Adventures in Wonderland*. It's kind of scary but I tell him I like it because I don't want him to think I am ungrateful.

There isn't a garden here for me to play in and so I get a bit bored and restless before TV starts. One afternoon I see a wall gecko running across the ceiling. I chase after it and knock over a glass on one of the side tables and it smashes to the floor. Mum comes running to see what the racket is all about. I feel myself shrinking under her gaze.

'Stop that at once! We are guests here. Do you want Paul to throw us out on the street!' I have never heard my mother sound so angry.

The house boy appears with a broom and dustpan. He sweeps up quickly and says, 'No problem, Ma. See I clean am. No worry.'

Mum thanks him, commands me to sit down and shut up, and leaves the room in a rage. I want to follow her. I want to lay my head on her lap and for her to rub my hair and make everything better. But I know Mum needs to be alone. I open *Alice's Adventures in Wonderland*. 'Who in the world am I?' says Alice, and I realize I'm crying. Alice chased a rabbit and ended up in Wonderland; I chased that gecko and all I did was make a mess and ruin everything even more.

Mum hardly speaks to me after that. It's like she has vanished inside herself. My world is like a tall building being knocked down. Nobody mentions Dad and I'm too scared to ask. I am losing my connection to my mother. My siblings are all far away. Do they even know what has happened?

It's the third day of her silence when Mum finally speaks. She tells me we have to pack up because we are going home after school. I sink my nails into my palm. I sit on the bed watching as she folds her clothes and places them in a bag.

'I don't want to go home.'

She looks up at me; her forehead creases.

'Don't be silly. We can't live here forever. Now hurry up and pack up your bag.' She continues folding a shirt and looks around the room.

'You'll go to Justine's house after school. I've spoken to her mother and then she'll drop you home. I'll be there. I have to go and sort out some things today – that's why I can't get you myself.'

I bite my inner cheek. I don't want to go home but I don't want to upset my mother now she is finally speaking to me again, so I keep quiet.

After school Justine's driver takes me straight home.

'I thought I was going to your house?' I say as the car pulls into the drive.

Justine shakes her head and smiles. 'I've got a swimming lesson at the club. But you can come and play tomorrow.'

I wave to Justine as they reverse out of the gate. I walk slowly to the front door. Images race through my mind – Mum on the floor, Dad kicking, the men in white – and my heart pumps wildly as I step inside.

The smell hits me first. Old Spice and something sharp like sweat. My dad. I hear a low sound but I can't see him. Then he emerges from the corridor like a ghost, wearing nothing but a pair of underpants. This startles me more than anything as my father never wanders around the house without his clothes on. He is arguing with someone but I can't see who it is. I turn and run to the garden. I crawl into a hibiscus bush and crouch, tucking my knees close to my chest. He has come outside and is pacing up and down the verandah. Mum and Peace are out, Sunday is in the boys' quarters and I'm too terrified to move from my hiding place to go and call him. I put my head down and start to pray because I don't know what else to do and Mum told me that God always listens when we talk to him.

'Please God, help me. Please God, help me.' I repeat it over and over again until I hear a familiar beep at the gate, the roll of tyres over gravel, the opening of the car door, Mum and Sophie.

I run out from my hiding place towards them. Mum raises a hand to her mouth, and she grabs me by the arms.

'Oh my god, what are you doing here?' she says.

I can't even speak, my chest moves up and down and all I can do is wail. I point towards the verandah and they see Dad, sitting in a chair now.

Mum pulls me roughly this way and that, looking all over my body for I don't know what, then she gives a sigh and hugs me close. Her tears mix with mine on my cheeks.

'Mum, come on. We need to get him an ambulance,' says Sophie.

'Take her inside,' Mum tells Sophie. Sophie holds my hand and leads me to the house. I can't help glimpsing back at my father. He is still sitting in the chair, but he looks different, frightened, confused.

Sophie pulls me inside and puts on a film. *Escape to Witch Mountain.*

'Let's stay here and watch this, pet.' She rubs my hair, gently squeezes my hand for a moment and then presses play on the VHS recorder.

I try to lose myself but I can't ignore what's happening outside. There is a scuffle and raised voices and when I look through the net curtains, I see two men holding my dad down as a third man injects him.

'Come here, Lily. Don't look.' She pulls me back to the sofa and draws the big curtains so the lounge becomes dark. She switches on a light and sits beside me on the sofa. She holds my hand and I notice how wet hers is.

*

It's just me and Mum in the house now. She's paler than usual and the shadows underneath her eyes are darker. She looks like she could sleep for a week but something is pulling her forward. Now she is on the phone telling people about Klausman, the businessman who came to the house that day. He stole Dad's money. I hide behind the sofa with my notebook and listen and make notes like I'm a detective.

Her voice is so calm and confident, it's like I'm not listening to my mum, but someone else, someone powerful and in control. I don't really understand what has happened but I know it is something terrible. And I know that Mum is saving us.

She stays on the phone for hours – even with the bank manager.

The next call is to somewhere called Interpol. I think it's some kind of police.

When she gets through, she describes Klausman. 'He is medium height, brown hair, moustache, blue eyes. No, I don't have any photos of him. He was staying at the Ikoyi Hotel. We haven't been able to track him down. I believe he left the country. The police here say he boarded an Air France flight to Paris.' She listens to the person talking and writes something down. 'Wanted in five countries? My God! Will you ever catch him?'

I draw a picture of Klausman in my notebook. Maybe it will help the police.

*

It's five days since they took Dad away and this morning Mum tells me we are going to visit him in the hospital. There's a sharp pain in my stomach when she says this.

'No! I don't want to see him!' I say, surprised by the power of my voice.

Mum bends down and presses her palms on my shoulders. They are heavy and I want to shrug them off. She is so close I can see her pupils. Mum has large grey eyes with little flecks of amber that show up when the light catches them. She always says she hates her eyes because they are grey and boring like the wet Irish weather. She wishes she had blue eyes like her mother. She stares at me with those grey eyes and my body shakes with the force of her.

'There is nothing to be frightened of. The doctors are making him better with their medicine. Your daddy can't hurt anyone now. But he needs to see us. He's very lonely and sad in the hospital and it would make him happy to see you.' Her voice sounds like it is coming through a tunnel; there is a tremble to it.

I ask her the family code for do you still love me. 'Are you my friendies?'

'Of course I am, pet. I'm your best friend.' She draws me close and hugs me and I am safe again.

*

The hospital smells like Jeyes and bodily fluids. As we walk through the ward Mum tenses up. Her eyes are red raw and watery. We pass several beds with men lying in them; some sit up and stare at us, one man waves at me. Finally we arrive at Dad's bed. He is lying in a sea of white sheets. His skin is so black, and puffy and blotchy. His mouth hangs open like a door and a line of drool slides down his chin and pools under his neck. His eyes are two slits. Long curly eyelashes. I can't tell if he is awake or not. I have been holding my breath and exhale slowly as I watch his chest rise and fall.

Mum is going through his bedside table. She has brought more things for him, his favourite Imperial Leather soap, some Old Spice aftershave, a box of tissues, a Tupperware container with egusi and pounded yam, some chopped papaya, and a few other bits and pieces. She arranges everything in the cabinet as though she has done this many times before.

Suddenly Dad's eyes flicker open. For a horrible moment, I see only the whites. Then the dark pools of his eyes roll down and slowly focus on me. He stares as though I am a stranger. I back away and collide with a trolley, knocking something to the ground with a crash that startles us all.

Mum kisses Dad on his cheek and talks softly to him. Then Sophie arrives. She greets my parents and they all talk. Dad's voice sounds like it's coming from the bottom of a very deep well. Mum places a hand on his chest and tells him to rest. Eventually he reaches out for my hand. I back away, I can't help it. A tear runs from the corner of his eye.

A man wearing hospital pyjamas comes over and introduces himself.

'I am Monsignor Okafor, bend and kiss my ring.' He holds out his hand to me. On one finger, there is a gold ring with a large red stone on it.

'Take her outside,' says Mum to Sophie.

Sophie guides me to the garden area. I look up at her and she smiles down at me. I like this new friendly Sophie.

'Aren't you scared of him?' I ask as we sit on a bench.

'Who? Daddy? No, not at all. You don't need to be frightened. He's going to be fine. He's been sick before and he got better.'

'But he tried to kill Mummy.'

She turns to me. 'No, he didn't.' She shakes her head.

'Yes, he did. I saw it. You weren't there.'

'You are just a child. You don't know what you saw.' Sophie's voice becomes harsh and urgent, and her face turns to stone.

I swing my feet back and forth and stare at the garden, a field of yellowing grass. Some people are wandering around in circles, talking to themselves. A man sits on the grass slapping his face with the palm of his hand. It makes a noise like an elastic band being snapped. Others sit on benches and doze under the shade of the trees. The sun is beating down. I look up at it and am temporarily blinded.

I want to cry but instead I try to make myself calm, like Sophie.

'Why can't we go home now?' I ask.

Sophie sighs and shakes her head but doesn't answer.

*

The days pass by slowly. I've made up a new game: banging. It involves playing music on the stereo very loud. I listen to Sophie's and Luke's records. Donna Summer, David Bowie, Earth, Wind and Fire, The Police, Billy Joel. Those beats are perfect for banging.

I sit on an armchair, fold my arms across my chest and rock back and forth in time to the music. The motion and the music work like a magic portal transporting me to another world. I control everything that happens in that world and it's always good. I go to Narnia with the Pevensie family and meet Aslan. He lays his paw on my hand and looks deeply into my eyes and tells me that he will always keep me safe. I take part in battles with Prince Caspian who is secretly in love with me and I ride my black stallion across snow-covered valleys.

I can lose myself in these fantasies for hours and the only thing that breaks the spell is a call from the real world. Or when the music suddenly stops because the electricity has cut out. This is usually followed by an angry voice from the kitchen.

'NEPA don't go!' This is what we say when the power goes out.

I wish I could stay lost forever in my banging world. The real world is too difficult to live in.

CHAPTER 8

Manchester, 1990

I had always been a little afraid of my father but after The Incident my fear increased tenfold. It was like I no longer recognized the man who came back from the hospital. My father had been stripped away and what was left was an empty shell. The most startling change were his eyes: where they had been bright before, now they were dark and glazed. His face seemed to have dropped and he developed a hunch; when he moved it was with a slow shuffling gait. I found this creature more frightening than the wild one that attacked my mother. I imagined my father was possessed and whatever creature had entered his body was still residing there. This made me distrustful and nervous in his presence. During that time my mother was distant, she was so preoccupied with looking after him.

Sophie went back to university and Maggie and Luke were still in England. There was no one for me to turn to. So I turned inwards. I retreated into my imaginary world and banged and when I couldn't play the music because Mum and Dad were in the lounge I banged anyway, I closed my eyes and rocked myself back and forth and flew across into the Narnia of my imagination where I was strong and happy and an important member of a group of friends trying to save the world. There I had control over my life.

Lagos, 1984

Dad is back at home now. He was in hospital for ten days. Mum says he's better, but he doesn't look better to me. He walks like a tortoise; his face has dropped – as though the skin is hanging off it; and his eyes are two deep wells of nothing. Every time I see him, I picture Mum on the marble floor, her hands splayed out like starfish, her legs all twisted and her face a mix of terror and hurt.

Now he's back I have to sleep in my own room again. I miss having Mum next to me for comfort. I spend most of the night reading until my eyes close and I drift off into a nightmarish sleep. I wake up in the morning soaked in sweat, at first unsure where I am.

I avoid Dad as much as possible. When I get back from school I go straight to my bedroom until Mum comes home from work. Today, Sunday prepared my favourite food, yam pottage, to try to tempt me to the table. That delicious smell of palm oil, crayfish and meat coming from the kitchen made my mouth water and my belly growl like crazy. But still I can't face eating alone at the same table as my father.

When Mum gets back from work, she wants to know why I've not been having my lunch.

'Are you sick? Come up here.' She sits on my bed and pats the space next to her.

She puts the back of her hand on my forehead.

'You aren't hot.' Her eyebrows crease together.

I study the white swirling patterns on my blue tie dye dress.

'What's wrong?' Mum asks.

'I don't want to see Daddy.'

'You don't need to be scared, pet.'

'But he tried to kill you.'

'No. He was sick.' She shakes her head. 'He's all better now.'

'But he doesn't look better to me.'

'You have to stop this.' My mother's tone is suddenly fierce. She stands up. 'I have so much to deal with, Lily. I'm not able to deal with all this from you as well!' She gestures roughly with her hand towards me, like I am an unwanted problem.

*

It's me, Mum and Dad for dinner. Dad can talk now and his eyes have lost that strange emptiness. Mum is sitting beside him holding two plastic containers with pills inside them.

'Why don't you take them earlier? Maybe you'd be less sleepy in the morning.'

Dad shakes his head. 'They don't work like that, Cara.'

Mum opens one bottle and tips a pill onto the table. She

repeats this with the other bottle but this time she takes out two pills. She hands them to my father who drinks them down with water, making a face as he swallows. Then he opens his mouth wide and shows Mum his tongue.

'Happy?' There is a nastiness in his voice.

He stares at me and points at Mum. 'You know your mother would make a great prison warden.' He studies his plate with a look of disgust. It's egusi stew and a ball of pounded yam. 'I can't eat this.'

Mum frowns. 'Why?' There is an edge to her voice.

'I feel sick. The medication is making me ill. My head is drumming against my skull. We need to speak to Dr Odeyemi. I can't continue with it.' He rubs his temples and squeezes his eyes closed.

'You know you have to take the medication, Obi,' says Mum quietly.

Dad turns towards her and I am convinced he is going to hurt her again. There's a rushing in my ears, lights dart behind my eyes and then ... darkness. Then I'm on the floor, my parents' faces hovering over me. They pull me up to sitting. I look at Dad's hand gripping my arm. The pressure is beginning to hurt. Everything is blurry around the edges. I touch my face to check for my glasses, but they're still there. Mum cups the back of my neck and gently helps me up to the table.

'Come, let's get you into bed.'

That night, she stays beside my bed. 'It will be all right. He'll be all right. It's going to be all right.' She repeats this over and over.

Tears slide down her face and, for the first time since The

Incident, I realize Mum can't protect me. She's more afraid than I am.

*

I am going to stay with Luke in England. Mum told me this afternoon, while Dad was asleep. Luke is living in a city called Manchester with his girlfriend's family. (He ran away from boarding school and won't come back home to Lagos.) It's all arranged.

'There's a little sister about your age and two teenage brothers. The father still lives in Nigeria. The mother is Irish.' Mum tells me this as though being Irish is an assurance that she will be a safe guardian.

At last! After the endless hours of boredom and loneliness I've lived with here, someone close to my age to play with. I'm excited. Everyone knows England is the best place!

I am slightly disappointed I'm not going to London, though. In the markets you always hear people say, *I'm going to England, London*, like London is a country where England can be found. Manchester is not a place you hear people talking about. I don't even know where it is. When I check the map in the school library, I find Manchester is a small black dot somewhere in the north-west. I use a ruler to measure the distance between the dot and London. They are quite far apart. None of the Enid Blyton books I read ever mention Manchester.

*

It's my tenth birthday. I'm still in bed waiting for Mum to come into my room and wish me happy birthday, give me a kiss and place a clumsily wrapped present in my hands. But she hasn't come to me. I get up and pad out to the dining room. Mum is sitting at the table having her porridge with the same distracted look on her face that she's worn since The Incident.

'Morning. Here – eat your breakfast.' She points at a bowl on the table.

I stand and stare at her, willing her to remember.

'What are you standing there for, come on, you'll be late for school,' she snaps.

Eating the porridge is like trying to swallow clay.

I spend the day at school in a bad mood. The teacher shouts at me for daydreaming and I burst into tears – which makes things worse. I have to stand in a corner of the class, facing the wall.

When I get home that afternoon, I'm surprised to find Sophie is there. I scowl at her and wait for her to shout at me – almost willing the fight – but she doesn't. Instead, she smiles and tells me to follow her to the dining room. There's a box on the table and she nudges me forward to open it: a birthday cake, with *Happy Birthday Lily!* written in pink and purple icing! She takes out a pack of candles and starts placing them neatly round the edge.

'And let's not forget these.' Sophie hands me two neatly wrapped presents.

I am so happy that I throw my arms around her waist and hold on until she finally pushes me away.

'Hey, are you trying to squeeze me to death?' she laughs.

I peer at the cake; it's covered in white frosting.

'It's peaches and cream.' Sophie smiles, swatting my finger as I try to scoop up some frosting. 'We'll wait for Mum and Dad.'

She sits on the sofa and I go and join her.

'How is everything?' she asks. I understand what she means.

I stare at my knees. 'I'm scared of him.'

'I know, pet, but you don't have to be. Daddy would never hurt you.'

The front door opens and I hear the click of Mum's heels. Sophie gets up to greet her and I watch them hug. Mum looks tired and as she slips off her shoes one after the other I notice how rounded her shoulders are, as though she can hardly hold herself up.

'I've brought Lily a cake,' Sophie says.

Mum stops, lets out a gasp, then turns to me.

'Oh pet, I'm so sorry.'

Her lips are quivering and I know she really means it, but I'm still burning with anger. It's not just about my birthday. It's everything. All that's happened in the last couple of weeks. My dad is awake and coming down the hall in his pyjamas. He smiles when he sees Sophie and she gets up to hug him. He closes his eyes as he holds her and they stay like that for a little too long. Then they let go of each other and Sophie leads him over to the table and the cake.

'Let's light up these candles, shall we?' says Mum.

Sophie brings some matches. Her face glows in the orange light as she touches the flame to a candle. Once all the candles are lit they turn to me. 'Time to make your wish and blow,' says Sophie.

I close my eyes.

I ask God to make Dad better and to make things go back to the way they were before.

Then I blow out all the candles.

Everyone claps and laughs, even Dad, and I wonder with a spark of hope if my wish is beginning to come true.

PART II

CHAPTER 9

Manchester, 1990

When I think back to how I felt when I left home I'm surprised by how fearless I was. I was completely convinced that it was the solution to all my problems. An opportunity to wipe the slate clean and start over with my life. I found it so easy to disregard my home, my mother, my father. In the initial weeks leading up to my departure it never occurred to me that I would be homesick, that I would miss everything so much that the missing would manifest into a physical pain in my chest. I had no idea what it would be like living in a different culture, with a new family. All the banging I had done had made me think it would be just like my fantasies, that I would have control over everything, and only good things would happen. By the time I realized my mistake, it was too late.

Manchester, 1984

It's early March and there's a tag around my neck that reads *Unaccompanied Minor*. It takes two whole plane rides to arrive in Manchester and by the time I get there I'm exhausted. One of the air hostesses helps me find my suitcase and guides me through to the Arrivals hall and I see Luke immediately – taller and thinner than I remember but still my beautiful brother. I run to him and he sweeps me up in a hug.

'Wow, you're so dark. Look at you. Have you been working in the garden?' He ruffles my hair. His girlfriend Zoe is standing next to him. I met her once in Nigeria at the Rec Club – she used to have long dark brown hair, but now her hair is lighter and shorter with blonde streaks in it. I've never seen a half-caste or black person with blonde bits in their hair before. It looks cool.

Luke introduces me to Zoe's mother, 'Auntie Maureen', and her two teenage brothers, Sean and Mike, all pimples, buck teeth and Afros. They snigger in a way that irritates me.

Then a girl emerges from among the group. She seems to be trembling. She has the same pale skin as the others, like raw pastry. Her features are straight, with small eyes, a button nose with a scattering of brown freckles, thin lips and a pointy chin.

'This is Martha,' says Zoe, as she pats the girl's Afro.

I am so overjoyed to see someone close to my age that I want to hug her but something about her hard face stops me. Instead, I smile. Her eyes travel slowly from the top of my head all the way down to my Bata sandals.

'Come on, let's go get the bus home,' says Luke. 'Look at your teeth, Lily. You're like a little chipmunk. Are you still sucking your finger?' He laughs and I blush so much that I have to look away.

It's true I have an overbite because I suck the forefinger on my left hand. Unlike most other children I know I don't suck my thumb. I curl my forefinger and stick it in my mouth and suck. It's such a lovely feeling, but now my finger curves to the left and is a bit smaller than the others. It's also lighter in colour.

'We'll 'ave to put a stop to that, dear,' says Auntie Maureen. 'Lemon juice will do the trick. It worked for Martha here.' She points to Martha with her chin. Neither of my parents made me stop sucking my finger so why should this woman who hardly knows me want to? Is she going to force me? I look down at my deformed finger and the urge to put it in my mouth is so strong I have to curl my hand into a fist and press my nails into my palm.

'Martha, say hi to your new roommate.' Zoe pushes her sister forward. Martha makes a small noise and shrugs her shoulders.

'Hiya,' she says.

Outside, a cold blast of air hits my face. I stumble backwards from the shock. The air is different, the wind whips breath away from me. I have to gulp at it with my mouth.

We pile onto a double-decker bus. I've never been on one before. It's orange and cream, not red like the London buses I've seen on television. Martha and the boys race upstairs and I wobble as I climb up after them.

When I reach the top of the stairs I search for Martha. She is sitting on the front seat. The bus moves and makes me lunge forward and I bump into her shoulder. She turns and glares at me as I sit down beside her.

The journey is amazing to me. We pass by green fields full of cows, horses and sheep. The cows are so fat here! In Lagos the cows are so skinny their skin hangs onto their bones. We come into the city where the houses are so different from the houses at home. Many of them are made with red bricks like dolls' houses. In Lagos a man in uniform and white gloves directs the traffic. Sometimes he dances like Michael Jackson as he waves cars through. Here, there are traffic lights and there isn't even any sewage in the gutters.

It's as though someone has stripped the world down to three colours, brown, grey and green. Even the people are a pale shade of grey.

Martha turns towards me. 'Is your dad a madman?'

I don't know what to say. My heart rattles against my ribs like a calabash.

'Never mind. That's what me mam told me – he's mad. So, you've come from Nigeria. I used to live there once when I was little.'

The change in topic allows me to breathe again.

'I 'ated it. It was cruddy. Hot and sticky. Full of bush black people. It was rank! This is a much better country to live in.'

Martha doesn't sound like the British people I've met in Nigeria; the teachers at my school or the pupils, or the expats at the club, who speak with what my dad calls 'proper' BBC accents – clipped and clear and like they are better than you. Martha says words I don't recognize and struggle to understand. She sounds vowels like she's spitting them out.

When we finally get off the bus, Luke tells me we are in Moss Side. This place is like nowhere I've ever experienced. It looks scruffy and wild like an abandoned pet. There are children playing in the street but they don't smile at me like kids at home do. They glare at me in a way that makes me move closer to Luke.

My new home is in the middle of a row of beige brick houses. The house is tall, with two floors. The top floor doesn't have any windows. The house is right next to the road. People passing on the street can see into the lounge. From the outside, the house reminds me of a very sad person.

Zoe and Luke lead me through to the backyard. It's a small concrete patch that looks more like a junkyard than somewhere I can play – messy with old bicycles, a brown-stained mattress leaning up against a wooden fence, a red sofa with rips in the cushions and foam pouring out.

Martha takes me to her windowless bedroom on the top floor. It's a box with a single bed that takes up most of the space and sickly wallpaper twirling with green plants and yellow flowers. She's pinned up some music posters: Wham!, Michael Jackson, Bananarama, and a man with long hair and makeup called Boy George.

'We sharing. 'Til Mam gets a new one.'

I wonder where a second bed would even fit.

I open my backpack and pull out Sindy, hoping to impress my new sister, but Martha makes a face. 'Sindy's bobbins.' She grabs my doll. 'Anyway, only babies play with dolls.'

'No!' I shout, as I watch her rip my Sindy's head off. She smiles at me, cruelly.

To my relief, I manage to fix Sindy's head back onto her body. I stroke her hair to make her feel better. Auntie Maureen's crow-like voice calls up the stairs. 'Tea time!' I look at Martha in confusion.

'What yah looking at me for, yah spaz. Come on, time to eat.' She motions to her mouth and makes a grunting noise like a monkey, then bursts out laughing. I follow her downstairs and into the lounge where everyone squeezes onto the two sofas.

'Here, sit by me,' says Luke. He pulls a cushion off the sofa and puts it on the floor next to his feet. Zoe and Auntie Maureen bring our food out from the kitchen. Zoe gives me a tea towel to spread across my knees and then passes a plate with two pieces of toast, baked beans and a fried egg. I've never had a meal like this before. I was hoping for fish and chips ... but I gobble it all up.

After dinner, tiredness catches up with me. I can hardly keep my eyes open and the sounds of the family surround me like a fog. All I want to do is sleep and I turn to look at Luke and will him to take me up to bed.

'Don't fall asleep! It's bath time. Let's get you cleaned up and then you can go to bed,' says Auntie Maureen. I follow her upstairs to the bathroom. The whole room is a creamy shade of green, like an avocado. I'm a bit worried as I watch her run the bath. We only have bucket baths at home because water is scarce, so this is almost sinful.

'OK. On with it, girlie.' Auntie Maureen gestures towards the bathtub.

'Are you going to give me a bath?' I ask her as I remove my clothes, a little embarrassed.

Auntie Maureen cackles. The others hear her laughter and Luke and Zoe peer round the door.

'The little princess thinks I'll give her a bath!' shouts Auntie Maureen.

Martha comes in. 'Wot, you can't even wash yourself?' she says.

'My mum always does it.' I am self-conscious and annoyed with all those pairs of eyes on my naked body, all laughing at my expense.

'Well, here you have to bath yourself. OK?' says Luke, who's standing by the door, studying the wall as he speaks. Auntie Maureen gives me a sponge and a bar of green soap and everyone troops out. I check the water with my toe and get in. I sit holding the sponge in one hand and the soap in the other. It isn't the nice Lux soap from home. It smells horrible, like medicine. I sigh as I scrub my at skin.

After I finish, I dry myself with the towel hanging on the radiator. It's rough and threadbare, not soft and fluffy like our towels at home. I change into my nightie then pad to Martha's room. Martha is already in bed. She's tucked in with the duvet up to her chin. I want to ask where I can get bottled water to wash my teeth but I decide against it.

'Can I get in?' I ask, as she has taken up all the space.

'Eff off!' she snaps.

I stare at her, unsure what to do, but then she shifts over and I get in carefully, making sure no part of my body touches hers, poised so close to the edge of the bed that I feel like I am hovering above the ground. Then I feel a sharp pain in my upper arm. I flail and fall out of the bed. From the floor I stare up to see Martha leaning over and smiling.

'Why did you do that?' I ask.

'Because you deserve it,' she answers. 'Spoilt brat in your big house with all your nannies and cooks and cleaners. Yah think yah better than us.' She moves back to her place in the bed. I climb back in, and lie rigidly, holding my breath until she's finally asleep.

Thoughts of home keep me wide awake. Mum and Dad are probably watching TV right now. I imagine curling up between them in bed like I used to do before The Incident. The sweet smell of her and the bitter tang of him. My chest hurts with this homesickness. I try to think of my favourite Narnia stories instead. I close my eyes and see myself walking from this cold tiny room through a wardrobe and into that other place. I see Aslan the lion, telling me to be strong, to have a fire in my heart, that everything is going to be okay.

CHAPTER 10

Manchester, 1990

Those first months in Manchester were the hardest. The fantasy I had built up in my mind of my happy new life was quickly replaced by a waking nightmare. I spent much of the time in a state of shock unable to react to my surroundings. I had thought school in England would be better, that the kids would be nicer and the teachers kinder. Nothing could be further from the truth. Most of the time I felt like I had been dropped onto an alien planet, everything was so different from home. This world was hard, you had to fight to survive. At the time I didn't realize that I had moved to one of the most deprived areas in England. Every day was a new battle. You couldn't show weakness or any kind of softness. A constant thought in my mind during that time was *How am I going to survive?*

Manchester, 1984

Auntie Maureen wakes us early next morning with a brisk clap of the hands.

'Did she take all the covers?' she says.

Martha is neatly wrapped up in the duvet like a boiled sweet. I'm huddled in a ball, with freezing feet.

Martha glares at me.

Zoe appears in the doorway, smiling sweetly. 'Girls, you have to behave and share. Come on now, it's time to get up.'

Breakfast is toast with strawberry jam. I love the saltiness of the melted butter with the sticky sweetness of the jam. It gives me a bit of comfort after a long cold night.

Luke and Zoe take me to visit my new school. It's about fifteen minutes' walk away. The whole street is one long line of houses, each exactly alike but with different colour front doors.

When we arrive, we meet the principal, a white woman with messy grey hair and dark shadows under her eyes. Her mouth curves downwards and she never looks in my direction. Once they have finished filling out the paperwork Luke and Zoe walk me out into the playground. It's playtime and the other children are running around screaming their heads off. Half of them are black or brown and the rest white. There are more black people in this school than at St Joseph's back home – this makes me feel better, somehow, as I don't want to stand out any more than I know I already do.

'You are going to like it here,' says Luke. He gives me a hug.

Afterwards, we go to buy my new school uniform. White

shirt, grey skirt, white socks. Not so different to St Joseph's, except for the red jumper we have to wear. The weirdest thing are the leather shoes, so tight and painful after the familiar freedom of my favourite Bata sandals which I'm still wearing (albeit with socks, to keep warm). Martha laughed at me when she saw them. I don't see what is so funny. I think this new 'sister' of mine is not only nasty but stupid as well.

*

I just want to go home.

Everything is so unfamiliar and strange now, and the pain in my chest keeps coming back every time I think about Mum. I even miss Dad. I can't believe how stupid I was to have wished so hard to get away, to have been so excited about coming here. At least back home, I knew the dangers. Here, nothing's safe. And Martha is *absolutely horrid*, as they say in *Malory Towers*.

Zoe dropped me at my new school this morning and I had to hold my breath to stop myself from bawling my eyes out. I've always had a problem with school. At St Joseph's I always felt trapped behind the school gates, where we had to follow orders or risk punishment. Now I have to learn a whole new set of rules and hope I don't accidentally break them. And it's even worse here because I'm joining in March, in the middle of the school year. Everyone already knows everyone.

I try to stop myself shaking as a teacher called Mrs Johnson leads me to my classroom. She is tall and thin with blonde hair tied up in a tight ponytail. She has large glasses that cover most of her face and magnify every blemish. The classroom is crowded and all the children are talking and shouting at once.

At St Joseph's we always had to be quiet when a teacher entered the room and there were only about ten of us in each class. Mrs Johnson points at a desk near the front and I sit down. I had hoped I could slink in at the back.

She puts her bags and papers down on the front desk and then walks over to the blackboard. She picks up a wooden metre stick and bangs it on the blackboard while shrieking at the top of her lungs, 'Quiet!' Her voice is so violent and high pitched I clamp my hands over my ears. The rest of the class ignore her and carry on shouting, playing, talking. She continues to bang on the board until the noise settles down. Then she says, 'This is Lily. A new pupil. Everyone say hello to Lily.'

Everyone stares at me. Some start sniggering. 'Hi-ya Li-ly,' they chant, in a way that makes me want to burst into flames. I shrink down lower in my chair.

Mrs Johnson walks over and hands me a book. 'WE. ARE. READING. *NANCY DREW* ... HOW. IS. YOUR. ENGLISH?' She shouts each word out separately, which makes the class laugh even harder.

I seem to have lost my voice. I can't answer, I just can't make a sound. Why would she think I can't speak English? Mrs Johnson's getting annoyed now, I can tell. I take the book. She thinks I'm stupid.

'Who's going to read for us?' she says.

The black boy sitting next to me raises his hand in a flash. Mrs Johnson narrows her eyes slightly and pretends not to notice, looking around for someone else.

'Miss! Miss! Pick me, Miss!' The boy actually jumps in his seat.

'Quiet, Winston. Stop disrupting the class. Put your hand down,' she says and continues scanning the room before stopping at a girl with curly blonde hair. She knocks the desk with her knuckle and says, 'Read, Emily.'

Winston collapses in his chair. His shoulders slump then he folds his arms across the table and rests his forehead down. I think he is crying.

After Emily has her turn Miss calls on a boy behind me to read next – Raymond. He's black, but he doesn't look like any black person I've ever seen. He has a straight nose, thin lips and curly hair. In Nigeria, we'd call it European hair or straight hair because it has no frizz.

Raymond opens his book. He stares down for several minutes with wide eyes, as though there is a large spider sitting on the page.

Then he starts. 'Thhhhhh booooooooyy hasss.' He takes a breath. 'Uuuuuh.' It's torture listening to him. His face is squeezed into a look of pain. Every time he says a word it's as though he has to scrape it out of himself with a knife. At one point he gets to an impossible word. Climbed. 'C-l-cliiiim-buh-d.' Beads of sweat form on his upper lip. I turn back around in my seat because I don't want him to see me looking.

He tries to spell out the letters individually. It takes a couple of minutes for Raymond to realize that all the children are laughing at him because he is so focused on reading, but when he does, something frightening happens. He changes. I hear the screech of his chair on the floor behind me and turn to see a different boy. He reminds me of that TV character the Hulk. He clenches his fists at either side of his chest, his cheeks puff out, and he lets out a roar like a lion. Then he picks up his chair and throws it across the room.

I am both terrified and a little impressed. It's as though he isn't present in his body because when I look at his eyes, they are glassy with an expression I have only ever seen once before. Dad. The Incident. A fierce pain strikes in my chest and I sink to the floor and hide under my desk.

Raymond runs around the room, wildly grabbing and throwing whatever he can get his hands on. All the girls are screaming, some of the boys are laughing, the teacher runs out of the room and I can't believe she has left us. Two men barrel into the room, alongside Mrs Johnson, grab Raymond and struggle to control him as he kicks and bites and wails.

'Come on, everyone, back in your seats,' says Mrs Johnson. I wipe the tears from my eyes with the back of my hand. How did I escape from one problem, only to be faced with this new version of the same thing? We continue taking turns reading until the bell goes and everyone piles out of the room for break.

I hide in a corner of the playground and pray no one notices me. But soon enough a small crowd gathers around.

'She's from Africa,' says a ginger-haired boy with rings of dirt around his neck.

'Do you swing in trees over there?' asks a big black boy with an uneven Afro.

'You live in a mud hut, don yah? I saw it on telly,' says a girl with a mess of blonde hair.

'She can't even speak English!' says a half-caste girl. This hurts because when I first saw her I thought we might be friends, as we look a bit alike even if her skin is lighter.

Then the first boy rushes towards me and pulls up my skirt so high it almost covers my head. Everyone points at my pink panties patterned with butterflies, and laughs. The sound of it fills my head – it's as though the noise is sand and someone is pouring it into my ears. I crouch to the ground, pull my skirt down over my knees and cover my eyes with both hands. I try to close in on myself like the mimosa plants at home, whose leaves curl up when you touch them.

Someone grabs me by the arm and pulls me up.

'Eeee RRR. Leave her. Move, man. Wot yah doin'?'

My rescuer leads me to a bench and orders me to sit down.

After a while I gather myself together and I look up at a tall girl standing in front of me. She grins and I see she has huge white teeth which are too big for her mouth. Someone has plaited her hair into cornrows.

She sits next to me and asks, 'Where you from then?'

My mouth has gone dry and when I try to speak nothing comes out.

'Is it Africa then? Did you really use to swing in trees there?'

I shake my head.

'Can you not speak English or wot, man? What's wrong with yah? Talk.'

'Yes, I can,' I croak.

'We're gonna be bessies now us. Innit?' She gives me a firm nod.

*

Her name is Gladys. Now she is my best friend she tells me everything. Her mum has *gone away* for a little while, so she is staying with a foster family until she gets back. Gladys hates her foster family because they are mean to her and have lots of rules; but she knows it won't be long until her mum comes to get her. There are two other children staying with the foster family and she says one is *a right psycho*. His parents are *druggies*. There is a little girl called Mollie. She's all right but she's always crying for her mum at night so Gladys punches her to shut up.

I study Gladys as she talks. She has a long neck and wide shoulders; she juts her jaw out and crosses her arms. When she looks at me, she holds her head up and squints.

'Where has your mummy gone?' I ask.

'To prison.'

'Can you go and see her?'

'No.' Gladys looks at her feet and kicks them back and forth.

'Where's your daddy?'

Gladys sucks her teeth. 'He's in London.'

I'm not sure exactly what this means but I can tell from the set of her mouth the question has upset her so I keep quiet.

'Have you got any money?' she asks.

I nod and fish out the coins Luke gave me for snacks.

'Give it 'ere then.' Gladys holds out her hand. 'It's all right, I'm gonna get us stuff from the tuck shop.'

I give her the money and she gets up and walks over to a little shop that I hadn't noticed before. She comes back carrying two small packs of biscuits and two cartons of juice.

She drops my biscuits and juice in my lap but I don't touch it. I can't eat. Gladys sucks loudly on her straw until all the juice is gone and the sides of the carton cave inwards. Then she turns to me and points at my lap with her chin. 'Are you eatin' that or wot?'

I shake my head and she grabs the biscuits and juice and shoves them in her coat pockets.

She lets out a sigh and says, 'Ticky it time.'

Suddenly she slaps me on the back and shouts, 'Tag! You're it. Run!'

I run for my life. Tag is one of my favourite games at home with Peace's children in our garden. But with Gladys it's a totally different experience. Gladys is bigger and stronger than Happiness and Hope put together but I'm small and light which makes me faster.

After a while she gets angry. She is sweating from the effort of running after me. I can see in the flash of her eyes and the way her lips pull back to show me those huge teeth like rows of houses in her mouth that I should just let her tag me – but my legs just want to keep running. Then I get a stitch in my side. I slow down to catch my breath. A hand slaps me on the back, with such force I feel my heart quake.

'Tag! You're it. Speccy four eyes!' shouts Gladys.

Just then, the bell rings for class. Thank god.

*

Every day at my new school brings a new kind of humiliation. I've only been here for a week and I hate it already. Today I learnt where the most sensitive part of my body is. A boy kicked me there at playtime and I fell to the ground and held onto my down there as though it would fall out. The pain was hot and

85

piercing and moved outwards in a circle. I squeezed my eyes shut against the tears, but they leaked out anyway.

The children love to pick on me. It's their favourite thing to call me names. They call me 'speccy four eyes' because of my glasses. I've been wearing them since I was seven and no one ever made nasty comments about them at home. Now, though, they're a bad thing and if I wasn't so blind without them I would throw them away in a heartbeat.

It's not just me. The Asian boy in my class gets called 'Paki bud bud'. There's a fat white boy who's called 'chubbers'. The two redheaded kids in my class are called 'ginger mingers'. The Chinese boy gets called 'ching chong' or 'chinky eyes' or 'yah wan sal vingar on chips' and then the kids pull their eyes into slits.

Here, being different makes you a target.

This afternoon I saw some black boys making fun of a black girl in one of the lower years. She is very dark skinned and has her hair in two puffs tied with pink string. She was clutching an old teddy bear to herself as the boys surrounded her like a pack of dogs. One of them kicked her down there. The girl curled in on herself like a hedgehog.

'Rosie, you're blik black! You need to turn around and smile! Yah nig nog golliwog! Blackie Rosie!' they chanted.

My insides hurt as I watched but there was no way I was brave enough to help. I walked away so I wouldn't see Rosie crying.

Many of the black children are from Jamaica. They look different from people at home in Lagos. They are all different shades of brown and some have soft hair like Europeans or they have small eyes and thin lips and long straight noses. They act like they are better than me because I come from Africa. One of them even asked me if I missed the jungle. Idiot!

I think they have this idea about Africa because of the adverts on the television here, which show pictures of starving African children, covered in flies and dirt, with round eyes and open mouths. In these adverts, the British man with his BBC English tells a short story about poor Fatima who has to walk five miles to get water and who doesn't get enough food to eat because her family is so poor. The advert then shows a village with mud huts covered with straw and lots of sad, skinny people standing around. Then the British man asks for donations of one pound a month to help.

*

I spend a lot of time here praying. In fact, I don't think I've ever prayed so much in my life. I pray to be strong so I can fight back. I'm constantly getting slapped, pushed, pulled or kicked. And that's not just at school. At home, Martha is always pinching my arm or she kicks me when no one is looking.

The kids at school hate the way I talk, they say, 'Are yah posh or wot?' But actually, the way that *they* speak sounds kind of funny to me and sometimes makes me want to laugh.

Also, I really hate Gladys. She steals my tuck shop money every day and if I don't do what she wants she slaps me hard on my face with those big ugly hands of hers. Once she slapped me so hard my glasses went flying off my face. I wish she would die and I'm not surprised that she hasn't got any parents cause she's such an awful person.

*

Something terrible happened with Gladys today. I was in the toilets washing my hands while she was grinning into the mirror, checking her massive front teeth for bits of food. Her eyes suddenly locked with mine in the mirror.

'Pull down your pants, go on then,' she said.

I stared at her.

'I said pull 'em down.' She grinned and pointed at my privates.

I shook my head and crossed my hands over my skirt down there. The punch came out of nowhere. It hit me in the belly and I curved into a semi-circle of pain.

'You betta do it or else!' she shouted, and to my shock she grabbed my skirt, yanked it up and pulled down my pants. At that moment some other girls came into the toilets.

'Look at her fanny!' she laughed and pointed at my exposed down there. The other girls squealed and helped hold up my skirt.

'Look, it's all pink,' said one girl.

Another one let out a snort and I felt her saliva hit me. The bell rang. My skirt was dropped, the girls hurried out of the toilet and I was left alone. I pulled up my pants, and as I left I caught a glimpse of myself in the mirror. It startled me. The girl I saw looked so different to the girl I still pictured in my mind. She looked older. Her eyes were hollow and her face was pale and sad. It made me think of the angel on the Christmas tree – take away all of her sparkles and she'd just be a tatty old piece of plastic.

I don't know how I'm going to survive at this school or in

this house. I want to talk to Luke about it but there's always someone else around and I can't say anything in front of them. I guess all I can do is wait and pray.

I've decided the best option is to make myself as invisible as possible. This evening, while everyone was out, I watched a nature documentary on TV. It showed an English man wearing a white shirt and khaki shorts in a jungle. The way the man spoke, quietly awed and whispering, I could tell he was excited. Crouching down, he pointed to a lizard that was sitting on a tree branch – a chameleon. This chameleon, he told us as the camera zoomed in, changes colour to protect itself from predators.

Next the camera panned upwards to show a large bird high in the treetop. The bird hopped from branch to branch, getting closer and closer to the lizard. The presenter described how the chameleon had already sensed the danger. It was like magic: one minute that lizard was bright green and the next it had blended into the tree bark. Invisible. The bird stood for some minutes, its head turning this way and that, then it flew away.

'A lucky escape for this little fellow,' the man said with a chuckle. I exhaled.

I need to become a chameleon.

*

I test it out in the playground. Standing against a wall, I close my eyes. *Be a chameleon, be a chameleon.* A nice feeling washes over me and I'm thinking, maybe I've done it! I've made myself invisible!

'Lily, wot you doin'? Oi! Wot's up with yah?' It's her.

I keep my eyes closed. I know what's coming. The slap makes my bottom teeth jar against the roof of my mouth. I hold my cheek and glare at Gladys.

'Come on, let's play skippin'.' She pulls me by the hand and I follow. The girls have two skipping ropes and one is jumping in between them. The ropes swish as they move through the air. I've never seen anyone skip like that. It's beautiful.

'You wanna try?' says Gladys.

'I don't know how.'

'You can start with one rope.' She raises her hand and the girls let the ropes drop. They use one rope and swing it in wide circles.

'Come on, jump in!' shouts Gladys. At first I worry this is some awful trick but I hold my breath and jump in and start skipping. I find my rhythm and for the first time since I arrived in this place I feel free. I can't stop laughing and smiling, it's like flying, and when the bell goes I am disappointed we have to stop.

'Will you teach me how to do it with two ropes?' I ask Gladys.

'Sure,' she smiles and pats me on the shoulder.

Maybe she's not as bad as I thought.

CHAPTER 11

Manchester, 1990

I had expected to fit neatly into the family like the missing person they had all wished for. The reality was very different. I realize now they were suddenly lumbered with a young child. Auntie Maureen was a single mum struggling to make ends meet, stretching out her benefits money every week, trying to keep control of her two teenage sons who had turned wild. On top of that my brother was already living with her. And yet she never made me feel unwelcome. She treated me like part of her family. But I expected her to be the same as my mum, and because she wasn't, I grew to dislike her. The family was loud and boisterous and playful. So unlike my own. I was used to solitude and silence, to being ignored. In this family I drew unwanted attention and I soon realized that my biggest problem was going to be Martha.

Manchester, 1984

Auntie Maureen is queen of the castle. She's the one the others look to for permission, the only one they listen to. For the most part she just smiles or laughs everything away. Nothing seems to bother her, not even the two boys fighting. They look like they're trying to kill each other with their bare hands – she calls it 'rough play'.

I've made a list comparing Auntie Maureen and Mum because the longer I stay in this place the more likely it seems that Auntie Maureen is going to be my new mum. I can tell that they had different starts in life. To begin with, Mum's Irish accent is nicer – softer, gentler. Mum wears much fancier clothes and jewellery. Mum is tall and slender, elegant like a swan. She has long slim fingers and used to play the piano. My mum likes having cocktail parties and reading. Auntie Maureen is completely different. Her accent is so strong I sometimes can't understand what she says. She is short and round like an apple. She wears t-shirts and a pair of faded jeans (my mum would never!), and I don't think parties ever happen here. The only books I have found in this house are some dusty old recipe books, but there are loads of women's magazines and Auntie Maureen reads them on the sofa, licking her finger to turn the pages and chuckling to herself.

My mum comes out better on the list and this makes me proud and sad at the same time.

There *is* something that my mum and Auntie Maureen have in common, though. Drinking. My mother likes drinking Martini and Auntie Maureen likes drinking cider or beer. It's amazing how similar they look when they've had a drink: their faces become looser, their mouths hang open a little, they both laugh easily and their eyes become shiny and round.

*

Zoe taught me how to do my hair. I have to wash it first so it's good and wet, then apply coconut oil and comb it through with the Afro comb. The first time she does it, I expect the same painful ordeal as when Mum tugs at my dry hair with her brush – but it's totally different. The comb slides easily through my hair. It even forms curls while it's wet. Zoe rubs another cream through my hair. 'This will keep your curls in place.'

I close my eyes as she works her fingers gently across my scalp. It's the loveliest feeling in the world. When she's finished, I look at myself in the mirror and, for the first time in as long as I can remember, squeal with delight at who I see. My hair is curly – there isn't even a hint of frizz! Even Luke notices and says I look really nice. This makes me feel so special. It only lasts two days; by the third day my hair is back to being a sweeping brush of frizz. But it doesn't matter. That feeling of joy while Zoe was doing my hair was so beautiful and special and it made me realize that even when things are absolutely awful, there can still be these tiny pockets of happiness that come along unexpectedly like a butterfly landing on your hand. When I'm feeling sad and scared I'm going to remember that moment.

*

Martha goes to morris dancing class every week, and today I went with Auntie Maureen to watch. The girls wear dresses

93

that spread out like umbrellas at the waist when they twirl and smart black shoes that tap like clogs on the wooden floor. The girls dance in line and they are all white apart from Martha who is so pale she might as well be. It's amazing to see them move – all the action happens in the legs. I asked Auntie Maureen if I could learn, but she said I was too young. This is a lie.

Martha is like a different person when she dances, happy and glowing. She likes to practise her steps in the backyard. Sometimes I copy her and she laughs and tries to show me how. I like it. She isn't mean. I've discovered morris dancing and George Michael are the keys to Martha's heart.

*

It's a Saturday and Auntie Maureen, Martha and I are in the Arndale Centre – it's a big shopping mall and I love it there because we don't have Chelsea Girl, Top Shop, BHS and C&A back home and the clothes are all so pretty. Martha sees a skirt she likes and Auntie Maureen chooses one for me too and buys them both. Maybe she won't be such a bad mum after all. Then Martha and I have to wait for her while she goes into the shoe shop. We stand around feeling a bit silly for a while until suddenly she comes walking out of the shop towards us.

'Come on,' says Martha as she pulls me by the hair, 'hurry up.' Someone behind us shouts, 'Oi!' and Auntie Maureen and Martha start running. I race to catch up with them. We run all the way out of the Arndale to Piccadilly Gardens until Auntie Maureen slows down, looks around and starts laughing. Then she pulls a shoe out of her bag. 'Look at this!' she says; her face is all flushed and her eyes are sparkling like she's just won a prize.

'Oh, nice one!' says Martha.

I stare at the single shoe, blue with a low heel. 'Where's the other one?'

Auntie Maureen laughs. 'I didn't have time; we'll have to come back next week for that.' She puts the shoe down and tries it on.

'Fits perfectly,' she says as she twirls her foot this way and that.

'It's well nice, Mam,' says Martha.

As we sit on the bus heading out of town, I think about what just happened and realize I have another thing to add to my list of comparisons: Auntie Maureen is not nearly as clever as my real mum. As hard as I try to find reasons to think the best of my new life, I just keep finding reasons to be disappointed.

*

The sweet shop on the corner of our street is a place of wonders, with shelf upon shelf of huge plastic containers filled with all kinds of goodies. Fizzy Cola bottles, Refreshers, cherry Bon Bons, Love Hearts! But my favourites are the Flying Saucers, like papery Holy Communion wafers but with a fizzy sherbet that bubbles deliciously in your mouth.

In the shop I grab a paper bag, fill it with treats and hand the bag to the Indian shopkeeper behind the counter, who weighs it. 'That's 50p.'

As I count out my coins I realize I am 10p short and start to feel nervous until Martha appears at my side and places 10p on the counter. The shopkeeper takes it and hands me my bag. I stare at Martha in confusion.

'Wot you looking at? Come on!'

We eat our sweets as we walk back. I pop a Flying Saucer onto my tongue and let it melt until, delightfully, the tangy sweet taste of sherbet takes over. I look at Martha and feel happy. Another special moment to savour.

At home, I never really thought about money or where it came from. I didn't get pocket money because everything I needed was always there. If I wanted something, I just had to ask and someone gave it to me. Here things are different. There is never enough, even though Mum sends an allowance every month. We have a meter for our electricity and sometimes there aren't enough coins to keep it on. On those evenings I wear several layers of clothes in bed but never really feel warm.

Another way I can tell when the money is running out is what we eat. If it's sliced white bread, baked beans, biscuits, crisps, cornflakes and lots of cups of sweet tea, I know Auntie Maureen is 'tightening the belt'. The end of the week is always the worst, as we live on the benefits. They come weekly on a Monday – which means Monday nights are like a celebration, with takeaway fish and chips or Jamaican patties. Auntie Maureen buys her cigarettes and beer for the week, sits on her chair in the lounge in front of the TV and drinks straight from the can.

Each week Luke drops a 50p coin into my palm and tells me that's my money for the week. 'Be careful how you spend it.' Luke says he's going to buy me one of those piggy banks to keep my coins safe – I'm saving them for the coldest winter nights so I will be ready when the meter needs feeding.

CHAPTER 12

Manchester, 1990

I saw Martha the other day on a bus. I was walking along Oxford Road and there she was sitting on the top deck waving and smiling at me. My heart gave a lurch and I started to shake but instinctively I waved back and the moment passed as the bus moved off. All these years later she looks like a different person – prettier, kinder. And yet she still has the power to make me want to curl in on myself. I often wondered why she was so mean to me – maybe she was jealous of the attention I got. But the way she looked at me from the bus, there was love there, in her eyes, I could feel it. Maybe my memories are faulty; what if I've misinterpreted everything and she didn't really hate me? But when I think back, the events unspool in my mind like a piece of red yarn on a white background – sharp and crisp. And my chest tightens when I remember.

Manchester, 1984

I've been here for over a month now. It's April and the weather is still wet, windy and cold. I didn't know it was possible for the cold to get inside you. No matter how many layers I put on I can't keep it out. Me, Martha and two of her friends are sitting in the backyard on the green plastic chairs eating bowls of Angel Delight. When I finish eating I place the bowl on the ground. There are dandelions growing through the slabs of concrete. I go over and pick one of the yellow flowers. Behind me, I hear whispering and giggling; I grip the flower tightly.

'Oi, come 'ere,' calls Martha.

My heart jumps when I hear her voice. I've learnt the hard way. She tells me to take off my coat and roll up the sleeve on my right arm. Her two pimply white girlfriends nod and grin. I flinch as they both hold my arm steady and Martha produces a lighter from her pocket.

'Go on, do it!' says one girl.

The other girl elbows her friend and laughs.

They watch me the same way I used to study the insects in our garden, fascinated. Martha flicks on the lighter and moves it towards the skin on the back of my wrist. At first, there is pleasant warmth and I think maybe it isn't going to hurt that much; but then I feel the burn. She brings the flame even closer and I try to pull away but the girls hold me tight. I start to cry and I'm angry at myself for this visible show of weakness. There is a horrible burning smell and it takes me a few seconds to realize it's my own flesh. I can't take the pain any more and open my mouth to scream but nothing comes out. It's as if terror has stolen my voice. Desperately, I look to Martha – her eyes are shining with what I think is pure joy. Rage rises in me then, enough for her to see something change in my face. She clicks off the lighter and smirks.

She grabs the edge of my jumper, leans in close to my face and says, 'If you grass on me I'll kill yah.' I stumble backwards when she lets go.

A small patch of skin the size of a penny, bright red and shiny, has formed on the back of my wrist. I run indoors to find something to treat the wound. Upstairs, I sit on the side of the bathtub, my full body shaking, and close my eyes and cry hard as I pour some nasty-smelling TCP over my wound. I find a large plaster, stick it on and sit, numbly staring at the avocado tiles until someone needs to use the bathroom.

*

Since the burning I try to avoid being around Martha if she is with her friends, because that's usually when she wants to torture me in creative ways. I wish I could tell Luke how unhappy I am, but he and Zoe are joined at the hip, and even when she's out, the rest of the family is around. I'm more and more annoyed that he has never thought to ask me if I am okay.

Sometimes at night when everyone is in bed I creep downstairs to the lounge and it feels safe enough to play my old game, banging. Even without any music I can still do it – I just close my eyes, imagine 'Pass the Dutchie' is playing and bang to the beat. I'm in love with the lead singer. I picture myself skipping in the playground like a pro, two of my girlfriends holding the ropes and smiling as I put on a show; and then the singer suddenly appears! The skipping stops, he holds out his hand towards me and we dance together, his arms around me, and all the other kids gather round and clap. One night I am so lost in this fantasy that I don't notice the lights are switched on and someone is tapping my shoulder. I see Luke smiling at me.

'What you up to, Lily?'

'Just banging.'

'Are you missing home?'

I nod and say, 'I miss Mummy.'

Luke studies his feet. He is wearing a pair of black socks. A large big toe sticks out of a hole like a little head.

It's the first time we have been alone since I arrived. This is my chance to talk to him honestly – to tell him about Martha and the horrible things at school – but something makes me hold back. What can he actually do to help me anyway? Luke behaves differently here than he does at home. He's quieter, less outgoing, more like a guest, so I don't think he is really comfortable here either. The two boys always make fun of him and try to get him angry by calling him names like 'wanker' and 'coconut'. And if I do tell him and he calls Mum, what then? They might send me home, and while I would give anything to be back with Mum I can't face the idea of being around Dad the way he is now.

Luke sits down on the sofa opposite me.

'What's that?' He points at the plaster on my wrist.

I take a breath. 'I fell down.'

'Did someone hurt you, Lily?' Luke is leaning forward now, I can smell cigarettes on his breath. 'Was it Martha?'

'No!'

'Look, Lily, you don't have to worry, she won't hurt you any more, OK?'

'No! Don't say anything! It will only make things worse.' I see Martha's face, her lip curled upwards saying *if you grass on me I'll kill yah*.

Luke puts his hands over mine. 'It will be OK, Lily. We are going to leave here soon. I'm saving up from my job at the restaurant for us to get a place of our own. You, me and Zoe. You won't have to share a room with Martha any more.'

A fizzle of joy rises inside me. 'When?' I ask.

'Soon, Lily, give me a few months and I'll have enough, plus with your allowance money we'll be OK.'

I imagine having my own room, no more Martha to torture me, and I sigh with relief. Then Luke goes quiet and chews on one of his nails.

'Has Mum spoken to you about Daddy?' He looks at me closely as though trying to read a book written in another language.

I stiffen at the mention of Dad. 'She only said he is sick. But I don't understand.'

Luke sighs. 'Yes, Daddy has a sickness but it's in his head. It's like when you had malaria and Daddy gave you some medicine to make you better. Daddy needs some medicine too, and a lot of rest and looking after.'

'And then will he be better?' I ask.

Luke looks at his hands. 'I don't know, Lily. He's very ill.'

I shiver.

'You know he wasn't always like this.'

I lean forward. He has that look on his face and I can tell he's thinking back to a time I am too young to remember.

'He was funny. He laughed a lot. We all used to watch films together and comedy shows. It was fun. When you were a baby he carried you everywhere, he wouldn't let any of us near you, he was so worried about you getting sick.' Luke closes his eyes and smiles. 'He liked listening to music. His favourite was a Cuban song. He and Mum would dance to it in the lounge. Mum and Dad were fun. They used to have cocktail parties every weekend at the old house. They would laugh and talk to their friends. They were happy. We were a normal family, Lily. I want you to know that.'

Luke reaches over and squeezes my hand then he gets up to go.

'Don't stay up too late, OK?'

I sit still in the armchair and think about all he has told me. It isn't fair that I wasn't part of that happy family. I've been cheated. I think about my mother and for the first time I feel a hot rage towards her. It's her fault I am trapped in this terrible situation. In fact, I hate both my parents. Everything is their fault. And as angry as I feel towards my parents, I miss them so much. It's as if there is a big hole in my heart where they once were. All my memories of them swim before me and I long to go back to the time when my mother and I would work in the garden, or when I would sleep in my parents' bed, or those special afternoons when Daddy took me to the Rec Club. I miss waking up and seeing them at the breakfast table, Daddy eating his pap and me and Mum having porridge. I miss the loneliness of home, I miss the absence of my siblings that I tried to fill. I miss Daddy, the way he was before The Incident, even with his strange moods and bouts of silence. And those rare moments when he would wake up and see me. There is too much anger and sadness inside me and soon I will explode like a volcano.

CHAPTER 13

Manchester, 1990

In spite of my unhappiness I got used to living with the family. I spent a lot of time observing them and comparing them to my own. In this way I realized that my family was different – not in a good way. I wasn't used to being around people who were so at ease with themselves. At home we were often tense because of Daddy and the time had passed for childish games between me and my siblings. In that family there was no father to fear and this made everyone happy and free. It was then I began to wish that my father would disappear.

Manchester, 1984

Three months have passed since I arrived. I've decided to make the best of it. If I am going to stay with these people I just have to find a way to get through until I'm old enough to leave. It feels like forever. Time here is like a solid, heavy thing and I am trapped in the middle of it – like a mosquito encased in amber.

Life is like trying to walk on a wooden balance beam with socks on. When I arrived, Zoe warned me to stay away from her brother Sean. 'He has a temper on him,' she said, and now I know what she meant.

Sean unleashes his temper on his siblings. He changes in the same way Raymond in my class did on my first day of school. I've seen him try to strangle his brother over things as little as taking something without asking, changing the TV channel or simply looking at him the wrong way.

There is something about the sounds they make when they fight that goes through me and makes me want to scream. I can't watch.

Even when the family aren't fighting, they are rough with each other. They joke around, pinching, punching, hitting or giving Chinese burns. At first it's like watching puppies playing, but as soon as someone gets hurt, you can feel the mood darken.

What's confusing to me is how, despite all this, they can be really soft with each other as well. After a fist fight, the two boys always hug. And no one ever wants to spend time alone and quietly; they always gather together. They practically live in the lounge, watching TV or playing board games or just simply talking. I miss my privacy and often creep upstairs for some space and solitude, but if they notice I'm not there they come and ask what's wrong and tell me to come down and join everyone else.

I think about all the hours I spent alone at home – how Luke, Sophie and Maggie never let me join in, how rarely we did things as a family and only ever played board games at Christmas – and I can't help wondering if maybe some things about this family are better than mine. At least no one ever feels left out.

Another thing is how they are always hugging each other, or ruffling each other's hair. Sometimes the boys lay their heads on Auntie Maureen's shoulder as they sit on the sofa, while Martha likes to sit on her mum's knee and cuddle up like a big ugly baby.

Seeing Martha and Auntie Maureen share this affection makes me think of my mother. She never kissed me as often as Auntie Maureen kisses her children. Now that I think about it, we hardly ever touch in my family apart from when I sleep in Mum and Dad's bed and when I'm sick – when I'm sick Mum always gives me a hug. But I have to push her out of my mind. She makes me too annoyed. She's the reason I'm in this mess in the first place.

*

In the evenings we all watch TV. Programmes we don't get in Nigeria. *Dallas* and *Dynasty* are my favourites, especially Krystle Carrington. She is the stupidest person on Earth. I don't understand why Alexis is always trying to steal her husband. What's so great about him? He's an old grandpa!

I crouch on a pillow on the floor next to Martha and she often pinches or punches my arm when she thinks no one is looking. She seems to get a strange pleasure out of hurting me. Tonight, we're watching a programme called *Roots*. I take my seat on the carpet and hug my knees to my chest. As Martha drops down beside me she accidentally on purpose shoves me in the ribs with an elbow. My body tenses and my stomach gets all tied up in knots as I wait for the next attack. Luke is sitting with Zoe on the sofa above us. I watch as the credits for *Roots* roll and then I get a sharp punch in the arm.

'Hey! Don't you punch her!' It's Luke; he's leapt out of his seat and is now standing over Martha. His nostrils are flaring and there is a tremble in his lips.

Martha snarls at him. 'Fuck off!'

There is a moment of terrible silence in the room and I am certain Luke is going to reach down and slap her but before he can move Zoe stands up. I glance at Auntie Maureen; she is sipping on a can of beer, a small smile playing on her lips, eyes blazing hot coals in her face, but she doesn't say anything.

'Hey, Martha. Enough now. Behave yourself,' says Zoe.

Martha folds her arms and I know there will be consequences for this later but I am still happy. Luke and Zoe sit back down behind us and I can hear my brother breathing heavily. He puts a hand on my head for a few seconds and I close my eyes and smile to myself.

My mood is soon ruined when *Roots* starts. From beginning to end that programme takes me on a terrible journey of suffering, watching a poor African boy's ordeals at the hands of his evil overseer. Tears fill my eyes as he screams. Martha holds her hand up to her mouth. Zoe starts crying. Mike and Sean become angry. Only Auntie Maureen seems unaffected. She just grins and says, 'The blood doesn't even look real.'

CHAPTER 14

Manchester, 1990

Like that chameleon I had seen on the TV, I adapted to my environment and eventually things did get better for me. I think the shift happened when I finally made a friend.

Manchester, 1984

It's June now and the playground bullies have at last lost interest in me. All except Gladys who still insists that we are going to be best friends forever. One more reason why I need to run away as soon as I am old enough.

Things aren't as hard as they were in the beginning. I don't know. Maybe it's because I know what to expect now.

At playtime I usually sit in a corner and draw. At the moment, I'm drawing a squirrel eating a nut.

'Wot yah doin'?'

My body tenses and I ready myself.

'Drawing,' I reply without looking up.

'It's dead good that. I'm Bev by the way.' I see a girl with tight cornrows, a barrel-shaped body and thick arms. 'Can I sit with yah?'

I nod.

'Show me how.' She points at my drawing.

I turn the page over to a fresh one.

'All right. Let's try and draw that tree over there.'

For the next few minutes, I show her how to form the outline of the trunk, the branches, the leaves and then use crayons to add colour and shade.

Then I hand her my drawing pad, turning over a fresh sheet of paper.

'Now you try,' I say.

I watch Bev work. She sticks her tongue out of the corner of her mouth in concentration.

'Can you play hopscotch?' she asks as she colours. She has a surprisingly soft voice.

'Yeah.'

She holds up the drawing and smiles proudly.

'It's good, innit?'

'Yes, it is. You can keep it if you like.'

She looks delighted, as though I've given her a gift.

'Ta!' she grins. 'Come on, let's go play.'

I'm a little nervous in case Gladys sees me but I follow Bev and we take turns to hop on the squares; and for several minutes I forget everything else. It's almost like having a friend.

*

Bev is Jamaican. Unlike the other Jamaican kids at school, she reminds me of people back home with her easy laughter and the relaxed way she holds her body, unlike the other kids who look constantly alert and ready for a fight. Bev makes me laugh, pulling funny faces and doing impressions. Being with her is pure happiness.

One day after school Bev invites me over to her house. Her grandma picks us up in her car. She looks about the same age as my mother and is quite short, with a round face and big round glasses with pink frames. She has the same barrel-shaped body as Bev but her legs are thin and her feet point outwards. She wears a wig of European hair, brown and wavy. From the back seat I can see the tight curls of her real hair peeking through at the nape of her neck. There is a pleasant waft of coconut oil.

After a while, I realize I don't know where we are and start to panic.

'Where are we going?' I try to keep the fear out of my voice.

'Whalley Range. Yuh nar kno?' Bev's granny speaks with a beautiful accent that lilts up and down like waves on the sea. 'Dis place call Whalley Range.'

'But how am I going to get home?'

'Nar worry. Me cayn tek yuh home, dear. Yuh kno weh yuh live?'

'It's near the school. I can show you.'

'Everyting sweet now,' Bev's granny says in her sing-song voice.

Bev lives on the ground floor of a big yellow house divided into small flats. When we get out of the car, Bev points her nose up in the air and says, 'Once a royal family lived in the whole house.'

'You mean the Queen lived here?'

Bev nods. 'Yep, she sure did at one time. Then one of her family moved in. Aristocrats they called.'

I stare up at the house. It's big but still not as big as my house in Nigeria.

Dinner is amazing. Bev's granny gives me a toothy grin as she puts a steaming plate of food in front of me and I gobble it up so fast I nearly choke.

'Yuh like dat curry goat?' she asks with a smile. 'Slow down, pickney! Them nuh dem feed yuh at home?' She raises her pencilled eyebrows.

I nod and try to slow down. The soft meat melts in my mouth the way it does in egusi stew. I can't taste any palm oil but the saltiness and hot spices take me right back to our table in Lagos. We never have food like this in Auntie Maureen's house.

After dinner we go upstairs to Bev's room. She gets down on her hands and knees and pulls out a stack of magazines from underneath the bed. We both sit on the bed and she opens one of them. I gasp and put my hand over my eyes.

She laughs and pulls my hand down. 'Look at that. She's sexy. Look at her down there!' The picture is of a white woman, naked and with one leg in Cork and the other in Kerry – something my mother says to me when I sprawl on the sofa. Her private part looks like a man's fleshy mouth covered in hair.

'Look at her tits,' says Bev. Her eyes are wide as she draws circles with her forefinger around the woman's breasts. I don't want to upset Bev so I nod and smile and touch the pages, carefully avoiding the lady's naked bits.

'Where did you get them?' I ask.

'They were me mum's boyfriend. He forgot to take them when she kicked him out.'

'Why did she kick him out?'

Bev stops drawing circles and shrugs. ''Cause he tried to get into me bed one night.'

'Why did he want to sleep in your bed?'

'Dunnu. He said he was lonely. Mum was working. Sometimes she works nights. Granny was asleep.'

'What did you do?'

'I screamed. Granny came running, you should 'ave seen her. She bash him good over the head with a pan. Then Mum got home. She put all his things in bin bags and threw them out on the street.' Bev claps her hands as she says this and throws back her head with laughter.

'He begged to stay but she went to the kitchen and got one of the sharp knives. She says "I'm gonna cut it off, Benjamin!" He left after that. Never came back.'

A memory of Daramola's hand on my leg flashes across my mind and I shiver, suddenly feeling very cold. Why do they want to do such things to girls?

Bev lifts up one of the magazines.

'I guess Mum didn't know 'bout these.' She smiles but I don't smile back. 'Where yah mum and dad?'

'They're at home. In Nigeria.'

'Yah don't look African.'

'My mum's Irish.'

'Why aint yah with yer mum and dad?'

My heart tightens and I press my nails into my thigh.

'Because there's something wrong with my dad. He tried to kill my mum one day and she had to send him to hospital. But when he came home he wasn't better and I was scared of him. I didn't want to stay at home. I thought it would be better here with my brother and his girlfriend's family. But it isn't.' The words pour out of me in a rush. It's nice to tell her these things though. I feel lighter after talking.

'Yah miss yer mum, don't yah?' Bev puts her arm around my shoulder and something loosens inside me – like whatever holds me together stops working. My body is suddenly too heavy to hold up and I lie on my side on the bed. Bev moves up the bed and positions herself behind me. She wraps her arm around me and we lie like that together. Her breath is on the back of my neck and it's oddly comforting.

'Me dad used to beat me mum so he doesn't live with us no more.'

'Sorry.'

'Wot yah saying sorry for? It aint yer fault.'

'We say that at home when someone tells us something sad. To make you feel better.'

'I miss my dad, I only see him once a year. He's got a new fam and lives far away.'

She lets out a soft sigh. We stay like that in silence and then the bed moves and Bev climbs over me and jumps off the bed. She goes to a cassette player and turns it on. 'Billie Jean' by Michael Jackson plays.

'Let's 'ave a dance competition,' she says.

Bev twirls and claps and steps from side to side and I watch, impressed with the way her body can match the beat.

'Come on, Lily!' She pulls me to my feet and after a while I close my eyes and let myself get carried away, holding an invisible microphone and mouthing the words. Bev does an impressive moonwalk and I try to copy her but end up tripping over my feet.

'What's 'appenin' 'ere?'

The woman at the door is wearing the highest pair of red high heeled shoes I've ever seen. Her legs seem to stretch for miles until they reach the tops of her thighs where they disappear under a black leather miniskirt. She wears a black tank top which outlines the shape of her boobs. Her lips are painted red and she has lovely large brown eyes lined with black kohl. She has blue ribbons braided into her black hair, which drapes around her shoulders like a curtain.

'Oh! Hi, Mum, we just dancing.'

Bev's mum laughs, revealing the gap between her two front teeth – a sign of beauty in Nigeria.

'Show me wot you got!' Bev's mum kicks off her shoes and pulls Bev up from the floor with both hands and together they dance to 'Somebody Else's Guy' by Jocelyn Brown. I try to pick out the similarities in their features. It's difficult, but they have the same kind eyes. Bev's mum moves like the dancers on *Soul Train*.

When her mum leaves us, I turn to Bev. 'Your mummy's gorgeous. Is she a model?'

'Yeah, she is. She's also a dancer.'

'Wow.'

My mum was always much older than the other mums at my school. My mum with her big glasses, thin body, flat breasts, sensible shoes with never more than a two-inch heel, old-fashioned flowery skirts and shirts.

I wish she was more like Bev's mum. I bet Bev's mum wouldn't have sent Bev away to live in a foreign country if her dad was like mine. She'd kick him out and keep her daughter safe. I picture Dad sitting on the side of the road talking to himself. I see me and Mum driving past pretending we don't know him. This thought causes a ragged feeling in my chest.

Later that evening Bev and her granny drop me back home. I go straight up to bed and imagine what life would be like with someone like Bev's mum. The thought is strong at first, but after a while there is a painful ache in my stomach that moves up to my throat, where it forms a large ball and makes it difficult for me to swallow. I miss my real mum so much.

CHAPTER 15

Manchester, 1990

In Nigeria I was used to police checkpoints, to being stopped in our car and having a uniformed man point a gun at Peace and ask him questions. Peace would give the officer a dash and we'd be on our way. I was even used to the much feared mobile police units, or MOBO as we called them. They chased people in their jeeps and sometimes dragged people from their cars and beat them up. This was part of everyday life at home and I never questioned it. But when I thought of England I imagined English bobbies strolling the streets like Superman figures; in my mind they were polite and kind and helped people in trouble. I didn't understand why the boys in my new family, Mike and Sean, often called policemen pigs and talked about them with unconcealed hate. I thought

117

this was further proof that there was something wrong with those two boys.

Manchester, 1984

Auntie Maureen plays bingo on Friday nights. Luke is working at the restaurant tonight and he won't be home till late so I go along to bingo with everyone else. It's a warm and muggy June night. When we arrive at the bingo hall it's hot and stuffy inside. The smell of fried food, sweat and stale perfume hangs in the air. I like watching the man work the machine and call out the number of the ball that rolls out of a hole into his hand.

'Legs eleven, legs eleven I say,' he calls.

Everyone studies their cards like schoolchildren taking a test and crosses out number eleven with a pencil.

Maureen loves bingo. When she plays her eyes become sharp and shiny, her eyebrows press together with concentration, her lips disappear into her face. When she gets a number, it's like someone switches a light on inside of her.

'Winnie the Pooh! Forty-two!' calls the man. Maureen crosses out forty-two.

'Turn the screw! Sixty-two!' I scan the card and point at sixty-two.

'Good girl,' Maureen says with a smile and I am happy to be useful. Then Martha grips my arm and motions towards the exit and I know I have no choice but to follow her lead.

Martha and her friends have a plan. They are going to the Chinese butcher down the street to steal some crisps. I lean in close and listen, trying to make sure I don't miss anything important. It's nice to be included in the heist, even though I don't seem to have any particular role.

The butcher is behind the counter chopping up a large piece of meat with a cleaver. He looks up as we enter and I'm sure he knows what we are planning. In a flash, Martha snatches two packs of crisps, the others get a packet each, and then she shouts, 'RUN, man!'

We sprint down the street with the butcher giving chase. I speed up, running like the wind, my feet hardly touching the ground. I easily outrun the others. I don't know how long I run before I come to a stop. I can't breathe and have a painful stitch in my side. When I've caught my breath, I look around. It's dark and I'm not sure where I am. I'm on a busy main road. A man with dreadlocks is sitting on a plastic chair on the pavement singing to himself like one of the crazy men on the streets in Lagos. I try to retrace my steps but end up even more lost. Then it starts to rain. My glasses get wet and I squint to see through the water. What if I can't find the others? What if they forget about me? Tears run down my face.

A group of black boys stand on a corner, hoods up, huddled together, the light of their cigarettes moving around like fireflies. I decide to ask them for help but as I'm walking over a police van pulls up and several policemen jump out. The boys run. One of them is caught and pushed to the ground. The policemen gather round, raise their batons and start to hit him. I stand completely still and hold my breath.

The boy's face is bloody, trapped against the pavement by a heavy boot. He is making a horrible sound.

One of the policemen spots me and raises his baton in my direction.

'Oi You! Get away from here!'

They all stop and turn to look at me.

'I says out of 'ere, you deaf or wot?'

I can't move. Then I look at the boy and he mouths the word *RUN*.

Suddenly someone grabs me from behind and I scream.

'Gyal, wah yuh ah duh here? Come now, nuh stand here.' It's the man with the dreadlocks. He takes my hand and leads me off but I pull away from him.

'Wah yah duh out here alone at dis time of night, gyal? Yuh cyan si it dangerous? Weh yuh mama at?' His eyes are red and watery and he smells so strongly of cannabis I cough when he comes close. His skin is very black like Daramola's and I am afraid he's going to hurt me.

He sucks his teeth and shakes his head. 'Pigs beat on them black yout all the time. Now, tell mi, gyal, weh yuh mummy at?'

The word *mummy* causes something to break inside me and I start to wail. The man looks frightened.

'No, no, gyal, we ah guh find har, nuh cry. Weh yuh wa fi go?'

I sniffle and breathe through my hiccups.

'Bingo. They are at the bingo hall.'

'Ah yes, I cayn tek you dere. Nuh cry, mi wi tek yuh back tuh yuh mama.'

I wish this man *was* taking me back to Mum and not back to this life I have been thrown into. He takes my hand again and I allow him to lead me along the streets; I don't have the strength to fight. His hands are dry and rough and it's nice to hold onto something.

Back at the bingo, no one seems bothered that I was missing. Martha and her friends are sitting at Auntie Maureen's table. When I join them, Martha punches me in the arm.

'Yah ran like the wind!'

'Did yah see her! Like Speedy Gonzales!' says Martha's friend Joanne.

I turn to wave goodbye to the dreadlocked man, but he's gone and I am sad I don't know his name. I force myself to smile as I sit down quietly. I try to think comforting thoughts, but all I can think of is my mother. How much I miss her but also how angry I feel. I think about what Luke told me about my family, how they were happy until I came along – but what did I do wrong?

That night, I curl up in bed and pull my old blankie up close but it isn't enough to calm me. My chest tightens. I have to take short quick breaths. When I fall asleep I dream that someone is pushing a pillow into my face. I wake up gasping in the middle of the night. Martha slaps me across the face.

CHAPTER 16

Manchester, 1990

Moving to a new place helped. It gave me some space from Martha and that claustrophobic family. By then I also had Bev as a friend so things at school were easier. For a time I was almost happy. The ache for my mother, my father, my home never went away but it was easier to carry around with me.

Manchester, 1984

I swear it never stops raining here, even in summer. The rain is different from at home, colder and it comes at you from every direction. If I get caught without an umbrella, I feel damp for days. I am thinking how much I hate the weather in this place when Luke pops his head around the bedroom door and says, 'Pack your things, Lily, we are moving.'

Martha is sitting on her bed flicking through a magazine called *Seventeen*. She looks up and narrows her eyes.

'I've found a flat for me, you and Zoe to live in.' He says *me, you and Zoe* loudly and looks pointedly at Martha.

I take next to no time to shove all my things into the suitcase I arrived with.

The new place is still in Moss Side but closer to Whalley Range. From the outside it looks a bit dirty and I can't help but feel disappointed. The building is similar to Bev's, an old house with big windows and three floors. The paint is peeling and some of the walls are stained green. Our flat is on the second floor. As we climb up the creaky stairs I am hit by a bad smell. I can't tell what it is but I hold my breath until we reach our flat. Luke unlocks the door and grins at us, announcing, 'Dah da!'

The front door leads straight into the lounge. There is a battered leather sofa with gashes in the fabric and an armchair draped in a green flowery throw. An old TV sits on a table near the wall. It has two silver antennae jutting out of it and reminds me of a giant beetle. There isn't any other furniture in the room. I notice a large dark stain on the carpet shaped like a wobbly circle. It's reddish brown and looks like dried blood. I still can't get away from the smell.

'Isn't it great?' says Luke. He's so proud and happy.

Zoe and I look at each other. Neither of us says a word as he shows us round. There is a small kitchen area with a worktop and a sink, which opens onto the lounge and a tiny square of hallway that leads to the bedrooms. The first bedroom has a double bed in it; the second bedroom is a box room with a single bed. Both the mattresses are stained.

'You want us to *live* in this dump?' says Zoe eventually. I've never seen her angry before.

'Just for a few months, until I make some more money then we'll get something better. My mum even said she's thinking of buying a flat here for her retirement. She said we could live there until they move in.'

'Look at the mattresses, Luke, they are covered in god knows what!' says Zoe. 'Anyway I thought your parents lost all their money.'

'They lost their savings, yes; but they own two houses as well as the one they live in, so there's the rent from them. It's true they aren't as rich as they were but they definitely aren't poor. Look, we can't live with your family any longer. I can't have my parents see us all living together like sardines. We need our own place.' Luke's voice has turned hard.

He looks at me. 'Now you have a room all to yourself. No more Martha to bother you.'

'She likes sharing with Martha so I don't know why you are saying it like that,' says Zoe. 'You like Martha, don't you, Lily?'

I look at the ground and don't answer.

'Let's get you settled, Lily.' Luke carries my suitcase into my room and puts it on the bed. Then he ruffles my head and smiles and in that moment I love my brother so much I want to cry.

*

The room smells musty and damp (at least it's not a dead animal). There is a small wardrobe and a chest of drawers. I start unpacking my clothes and hanging them up – there are empty hangers in the wardrobe. It smells of strangers. I put a clean sheet on the bed and a pillowcase on my pillow. I can hear Zoe and Luke arguing in the lounge.

I am so happy to be away from Martha and her whole family. Even though the flat is disgusting I can breathe more easily. I know Zoe hates it, but I also know my brother; there is no way he's changing his mind.

After a while, I decide to go and find them. It's past dinner-time and I'm hungry.

'What's for dinner?' I look from Luke to Zoe.

Zoe is balanced gingerly on the edge of the sofa as though she doesn't want any part of her body to touch its dirty surface. Luke studies his shoes.

'Ah well, you see, it cost me quite a bit to get this place and I don't get paid again for a few days.'

I wonder what this means as I'm still hungry.

'We could get something from the chippy for all of us – here, let me see what I've got.' He counts out his money on the table; the change rattles against the glass. He shakes his head and turns to Zoe. She pulls out her purse and puts a pound note on the table.

'That's all I've got. My dole money won't come through till next week.'

Luke turns to me and gives a short laugh. 'Have you got anything in that piggy bank of yours, Lily?'

I bite my lip. I've just spent all my savings on a new jumper. I shake my head.

Luke looks at Zoe. Something is passing between them, as though they are communicating without talking. Then they turn to me.

'Lily, can you do something for us?' says Luke. 'The woman who lives upstairs. I met her when I came to look at the place. She's very nice. Do you think you could go and ask her for a pound? So we can get some dinner.' Luke gives another short laugh, and cracks his knuckles. The sound goes through me.

I follow the instructions Luke gave me, first door on the left, number 4. I knock. The lady who answers is very pretty and looks like she is dressed to go out to a party, in a short tight dress, tights that look like fish nets and shiny high heeled boots that go up to her thighs. She wears a lot of makeup and her brown hair is teased out around her head.

'Are you all right, luv?' she says.

'Please could I borrow a pound for something to eat?'

The woman bends down to my level and puts her hands on my shoulders.

'Of course you can, sweetheart. Are you all right? Where do you live?'

'In number 2. We just arrived.'

'You poor thing,' she says, reaching for a handbag. She pushes a five pound note into my hand.

'Here, pet. If you ever need anything you come and see me. I'm Dorrie. What's your name?'

'I'm Lily. Thank you, Dorrie.' I give her a smile and she hugs me. She smells of perfume. When she stands up I see

126

that her eyes are wet with tears and I feel a bit guilty for making her sad.

When I get back, Luke and Zoe are huddled on the sofa. She has her head on his shoulder and he has his arm around her. It strikes me how young Luke looks; his mouth is slightly open and his eyebrows are knitted together. I hold the five pound note out to them and they yelp with joy and jump off the sofa.

'I can't believe you did that! Actually begging for money!' says Luke.

I am a bit confused; didn't he ask me to do it? I don't like the way he is looking at me, as though he's just realized something about me. Something bad.

'I know, I just can't believe it,' adds Zoe, shaking her head.

I didn't feel bad for asking Dorrie for the money, but seeing the way they are behaving towards me, an uncomfortable feeling is working its way from the back of my neck up to my scalp. I go to my room and Luke goes out to get the food. He returns with portions of fish, chips and mushy peas and we sit in the lounge to eat. The flat fills with the smell of vinegar but I've lost my appetite. I keep thinking about the way Zoe and Luke looked at me. The word *begging*. I saved them and they act as though I've gone and done something bad? Yet again, nothing is fair.

In bed that night, I have to use my coat to cover myself as best I can; of course we don't have money for a duvet. If they think I'm going to go and ask Dorrie for one of them, too, they'll have to think twice.

CHAPTER 17

Manchester, 1990

When Luke told me my parents were coming to see me, I was thrown into a state of panic. Pure joy at being reunited with them was all mixed up with fear of being disappointed by them. The visit only made things worse. It sharpened the grief I was carrying inside me and reminded me what I had run away from.

Manchester, 1984

It's the school summer holidays. I sit in front of the window watching the rain form little rivers on the glass. I focus on one little river and imagine it's me as it zig zags and rolls down the window and then joins with a bigger drop – that's Mum and

Dad. They are arriving in Manchester today and I don't quite know how I feel about that.

Luke calls from the lounge to tell me to get ready and as I put on my jacket, my heart is racing.

'What's wrong, Lily?' Luke asks.

I concentrate on tying my shoelaces.

He kneels down to the floor so his eyes are level with mine and places a hand on my shoulder.

'You know Mummy and Daddy love you very much and they miss you.'

A rush of courage comes to me. 'If they love me then how come I'm never part of all the happy family memories? How come Mum never told me about Daddy being so ill?'

'Oh Lily. That's not their fault. It's just ... when you were born things were difficult. And Mum probably thought you are too young to understand about Daddy. They would both do anything for you.' Luke wipes his eyes with the sleeve of his jacket.

'If they are so great, how come you ran away from home?' My bottom lip shakes and fat tears roll down my cheeks.

'Well, that's 'cause Daddy wanted me to be a doctor and I didn't want to. All that's ancient history now, OK?' He looks at me closely and I nod reluctantly. 'Come on, we are going to miss the bus.'

Zoe's family are coming with us too. We meet them at the bus stop. Martha narrows her eyes when she sees me and I stay as far away from her as I can. I sit by myself on the bus, annoyed that they're invading this precious time with me and my family and wishing they would all just go away.

Maggie was supposed to be coming up from Tunbridge Wells where she's at boarding school but she's decided to spend the summer holidays with her guardian – an English woman my mother knows from Lagos. I was hurt and disappointed by this news when Luke told me. It's been so long since I've seen her. I think back to Christmas when we were all together. How happy I was then. And then I push the memory from my mind.

We join the rest of the people waiting in the Arrivals hall. My body tenses in anticipation each time someone emerges from the customs door. My hands are drenched in sweat. I stand on my tiptoes, willing them to appear.

Then I see them.

Mum pushing a luggage trolley, Dad walking slowly alongside her.

Mum anxiously scanning the large crowd, zoning in, finally breaking into a smile as she finds Luke.

I wait for her to see me.

When her eyes meet mine, it's like I'm in a spotlight. She smiles widely and waves; when she gets to me she bends down and hugs me. 'Hello, pet,' she says. I am overcome with her smell, with the silky softness of her hair, with the feel of her skin against my cheek. I close my eyes.

She stands back to look at me.

'You've lost weight,' she says, frowning, then looks up at Luke and Zoe's family. Her eyes travel around the group, taking in each and every one of them. I notice Auntie Maureen take a step back under my mother's studied gaze.

I see my father then, behind her. He looks worse than when

I saw him last – crumpled like an old handkerchief. His face is bloated and grey and he's visibly confused, and as I watch him I realize: he's *frightened*. This must be why Maggie refused to come and see us. Our father.

Mum goes to him, hooks her arm through his and guides him over to us, and as soon as she touches him, his face relaxes – and just like that, he is my dad; the man I remember.

They are staying in a big red-brick house in an area called Crumpsall. It looks much nicer than Moss Side. The house has a small front garden and there is a lawn at the back with a swing and a see-saw. There are three large bedrooms. We all sit in the lounge and it feels like there isn't enough air in the room until eventually the boys go out to the garden and I can breathe a bit better.

I watch Mum chat to Zoe and Luke and decide I want to make her jealous so I move closer to Auntie Maureen and lean my head on her shoulder like I've seen her boys do. Mum sits stiffly on the edge of an armchair, and waves for me to come and sit in the chair next to hers. I don't move and Auntie Maureen laughs in a way that reminds me of the crows calling to each other. 'She's very fond of me,' she says.

Mum's face is so pale that it's easy to see her cheeks turn red. After a few minutes she gets up and goes to the kitchen. I feel a mix of triumph and guilt.

When Mum comes back her eyes are pink around the edges. For a moment I think she is going to burst into tears. She looks up at Auntie Maureen and says quietly, 'Thank you for looking after her . . . I just couldn't manage, with Obi not being well . . . she was so frightened.'

131

Auntie Maureen nods and waves a hand. 'She's been no trouble at all.'

There is a pause and I notice how silent the room is. Eventually Luke stands up and says, 'Well, we'll let you get settled in. Lily, you're staying here tonight.'

Zoe hands me a plastic bag. 'I packed a few things for you.'

'But I don't want to stay.'

'What do you mean you don't want to stay? Mum and Dad have come specially to see you, Lily,' says Luke. There's a hardness in his tone that I don't like. Yet again, my brother has made up his mind and I know I can't do anything to change things now.

It's just the three of us. Just like it used to be. I scowl at my mother.

'What's wrong, Lily? Why are you behaving this way?' Her voice cracks and tears fall freely down her face now she doesn't have to put on a show for anyone.

My father suddenly turns towards me. It seems like whenever my mother gets upset he comes back to himself.

'Don't disrespect your mother,' he says. His voice is croaky.

I fold my arms across my chest.

Mum sighs. 'Come on, let me show you your room.' She picks up the plastic bag Zoe left for me and I follow her upstairs.

The room is large with blue walls, a double bed and a soft duvet with a pretty pink cover. It smells of fresh laundry.

'Let's see what she packed.' Mum starts pulling clothes out of the bag and stops when she finds my Mickey Mouse pyjamas. I grab them and change with my back to her. I get under the duvet and lie back on the pillow, suddenly very tired. Mum sits on the side of my bed and touches my cheek with the back of her hand.

'Are you going to come home, Lily?'

I sit up in the bed. I want nothing more than to go back home but I'm afraid – what if nothing has changed, what if I go home to the same mess as before? I couldn't bear it.

'I want to stay here.' The words are as heavy as stones.

Mum twists her rings; she wears her wedding and engagement rings on the same finger. The engagement ring is platinum, with a diamond and two small rubies on either side.

'Daddy is much better now that he's taking special medicine to help. Like when you were poorly – remember?'

'But what sickness does he have?' It's a question I haven't dared ask before.

'He got sick after that bad man took our money.'

'I don't understand. What kind of sickness is it? Where does it hurt?'

'It makes him feel sad and . . . Lily, it's very complicated. All you need to know is he will never hurt you. He's better.' She nods to herself. 'He's better now.'

Part of me wants her to tell me I'm coming home, make the decision for me.

I don't know what to do.

I turn to face the wall and Mum leaves, switching the light off as she shuts the door. I curl into a ball and hug my knees tight. My future seems like a dark tunnel that I will have to move through alone.

*

My parents have been here for a week already but things still aren't right. Today we are in town, shopping with Zoe and Luke. In BHS, Mum tries on a matching flowery top and skirt and comes out of the dressing room to show us all. Luke and Zoe make oohing sounds, my father nods and smiles. I don't look. Instead, I stare at a mannequin and pretend nothing's happening. Mum comes and stands in front of me.

'What do you think, Lily?'

The outfit is covered with lilac flowers, her favourite colour. It's made of a kind of silky material and is very pretty.

I shrug my shoulders. 'It's all right.'

She bends down and smiles. 'Let's get something special for *you* now.'

When she comes out of the changing room we go to the Children's section. I can't help myself getting swept up in the joy of buying something new. As we pay, Mum puts her arm around my shoulder and I let her hug me, although I don't hug her back.

As we go down on the escalator, I am feeling almost happy until Mum suddenly turns round and her expression changes to a look of horror.

'Obi!'

My father's struggling to get on the escalator. He looks terrified as he tries to grab onto the moving hand rail, and as he does, he stumbles and trips. Mum screams. We watch from the bottom, helpless, as he falls down the metal steps. Luke pushes past us and bends down to help Dad, splayed out like an injured animal. Together, Mum and Luke help him up. I think he's hurt his leg because he is limping.

Much later, we finally make it back home in a taxi and Mum gently leads Dad to their bedroom. I go and lie down on my bed. He is still so ill. I really will have to stay in this awful place forever. The feeling of aloneness and abandonment seems greater and more grown-up than my body. In fact, it makes my body feel smaller.

*

The day they leave, I refuse to go to the airport to say goodbye. Instead, I ask Zoe to take me back to our flat. When Mum hugs me, I go stiff in her arms.

As we walk away, I turn to look back at her one last time.

Her face like the surface of the sea during a storm.

Her arm looped through Dad's.

Dad, frightened and confused.

My heart, flat and fragile as a piece of paper.

*

After that, time passes. The summer holidays go by. It's a relief not to have to go to school for a while. But it doesn't make much difference to how I feel. I shut myself down so well I hardly notice the days go by. I am surprised when Luke tells me it's September. Once again I go to school. I come home. I change my skin to fit in. At school I smile at Bev; I even smile at Gladys. At home I smile at Luke and at night I curl up and think about how my future is a dark place that I don't want to go to.

Sometimes I am forced to visit Martha and even when she pokes me I don't take the bait; I fold inwards until I can't even feel her punches.

Then in November the news arrives. In the end, Zoe is the one who tells me.

'Your daddy is very sick,' she says. 'Even more sick than before. Your flight back home is already booked.'

I nod and run to my bedroom, slowing at Luke's room – the door's shut but inside I can hear him. It reminds me of the noise the rams make back in Lagos, just before their throats are slit for Sala. I press my hand against the door, send love across the barrier to my brother.

I pack my suitcase and, guilty, smile because my wish has come true: the decision has been made for me. I'm getting out of here.

And then a coldness shivers up my back and across my scalp. *I'm sorry, God, that I'm happy Dad is sick. I didn't mean to be evil like that. Please God, help my father. Please don't let him be in pain. I'm really sorry. I will give up going home if it means you can make him better.*

Our Father, who art.

Our Father.

Our Father.

*

On my last day of school, without really planning to, I do something brave.

At home time I wait for Gladys at the gates. I wait patiently until she sees me, until I know she's about to launch at me as usual. Then, I do it.

136

'You are ugly and evil and I hate you and I hope you rot in hell!'

The words just come out. Stronger and louder than I've ever heard myself.

What happens next happens in a blur. Gladys's face goes from shock to fury in a second. She bares her teeth. *She's going to kill me*, I think, and I start running for my life.

She chases me all the way home but I'm fast and I make it through the door before she can lay her hands on me. I lock it tight and rush up the stairs to our flat. I run to the lounge and go to the window. There she is outside looking up at me, fists balled, eyes wild. I stick two fingers up at her, something I've learnt from Martha. Gladys goes berserk.

'I'm going to mess you up!' she shouts. 'You're dead meat!'

Zoe comes in and peers out the window. Gladys is pulling at her own hair in rage.

'What the hell? Who is that?'

'She's in my school.'

'Well, she can't be here screaming like a maniac.' Zoe opens the window. 'Hey, you, get the hell out of here!' she yells. 'Go on, go home!'

Gladys glares up at me and then backs away, her eyes locked with mine. I don't look away: I hold my gaze until she turns the corner.

And then I pump the air with my fist in absolute exhilaration.

Zoe looks worried. 'Are you all right, Lily?'

'I'm fine,' I laugh. 'Everything's fine now.'

And I honestly think it is.

PART III

PART III

CHAPTER 18

Manchester, 1990

Even though I couldn't admit it to myself, I was finally getting what I had been longing for since I'd arrived in Manchester. I was going home. I was frightened when Zoe told me my father was dying, the way she sat me down, held my hand and stared into my eyes. The way her voice went soft and low. From this I knew that what I would be facing on the other side of the world would be terrible. But there was a kind of peace that came with that knowledge; deep inside me I could feel it rising, a calmness at my centre.

Lagos, 1984

As the plane bumps along the runway, everyone claps and cheers. I wear my *Unaccompanied Minor* tag around my neck. Eventually the air hostess comes to find me and I follow her to the exit. Outside, the heat – even at night – hits me with force. After so long in the cold, I had forgotten this feeling and for a moment my head is dizzy with it. We go to the front of the queue at passport control. The officer smiles and stamps my passport. At the baggage reclaim I stare at the life teeming around me, trembling with it all: women wearing patterned wrappers, headscarves and bubas, babies tied to their backs with cloth; men in traditional kaftans and loose trousers; the sound of pidgin English, Yoruba, Igbo, Hausa and more.

The air hostess finds my suitcase and puts it on a trolley. She guides me out into the Arrivals hall where my mother, Sophie and her boyfriend Fela are waiting for me. Mum is wearing the lilac outfit she bought in Manchester. I rush towards them.

Mum hugs me. 'My pet, you've come home.' She bends down, puts her cheek on mine and brushes it back and forth.

'My god, look how big you've grown, Lily!' says Sophie as she strokes my hair.

Mum thanks the air hostess and puts her hand on my shoulder as we leave.

The drive home from the airport takes half an hour. The night sellers are out, squatting along the roadside with their kerosene lamps blazing and food frying. I wind the window down and inhale deeply – the smell, of akara balls and suya, makes my mouth water and my belly moan.

My parents have moved to a new house, in a different area, Apapa. The compound is hidden from view by a cement wall topped with shards of broken glass. A black iron gate at the entrance opens onto a short driveway lined with palm trees. As I get out of the car I hear the trill of the crickets and there's a strong floral scent in the thick night air. I slap a mosquito from my arm. Although I'm quite relieved not to have to walk into the old place again, with all its memories of The Incident, the lack of familiarity in this new place, yet another new home, makes me anxious.

Mum and Sophie guide me straight upstairs to see my father. We walk silently into his room where he is lying in his bed. The air smells earthy, musty, of illness. Mum tells me my father has had a stroke. He cannot walk or talk. I approach the bedside. His mouth falls downward into his chin and his nose has merged with his cheeks. What stands out are his eyes. They have changed colour. They are dark blue. I have heard all babies have blue eyes when they are born and wonder if our eyes revert to this colour when we get ready to leave.

I don't really understand what a stroke is but as I look at him I understand he will never recover. I stand and hold his hand and he looks straight at me, with recognition, with a kind of knowing. He is trying to tell me something.

Mum points to a large double bed next to Dad's. 'We'll sleep here, Lily.'

*

It is just me, Mum and Dad. I lie in bed nuzzled up to Mum, wearing my old Mickey Mouse pyjamas. It's an exquisite happiness, as if every tension I've held in my body this past year has suddenly loosened and left me in peace. I fall into a deep sleep with her arms wrapped around me.

A moaning noise wakes me and I sit up, alert. Mum is standing by Dad's bed. When she sees I am awake she asks for my help.

'We need to roll him, so his bed sores don't get worse.'

I stand next to her as she pulls the covers off Dad. I see he has his pyjama top on and on the bottom he's wearing a nappy.

'Here.' She shows me where to put my hands on his hip. 'Let's roll him.'

We roll him onto his side and he lets out a wail that makes me gasp. 'Are we hurting him?'

Mum nods. 'We have to do this to make him comfortable. It's all right. Now hold him.'

I hold his hip. His skin is loose and wrinkly and just hangs to his skeleton. The hardness of bone beneath my fingers makes me want to retch. I look up at his face. He is watching me, tears in his eyes. His lips are wobbling. I look away because I'm afraid I will lose my grip on him. Mum is taking off his nappy so I stare at a painting on the wall. It's a landscape of billowy clouds, a mountain range, forests and a lake. It has been with us forever and the familiarity of it calms me.

A movement catches my eye. I look down to see Mum dabbing iodine onto Dad's bedsore. It's like a cavern in his left buttock, as though an animal has taken a chunk out of him. The flesh is pink, turning yellow at the centre.

'Don't look, Lily,' says Mum and I force myself to turn away again. Dad groans as Mum cleans the wound.

'Now we wait a little while. So the sores can air,' says Mum.

We stand like that for what seems like hours. I stare at the painting to protect Dad's dignity. Then, gently, Mum starts to put a new nappy on him.

'Right, all done. Let's get some rest.'

Back in bed I can't fall asleep; I can still hear Dad, quietly whimpering like a wounded creature. After a while he settles, and the moans become little snores. Mum is breathing heavily next to me. I lie like that all night, awake between my sleeping parents.

In the morning, I meet my father's nurses. One of them, an elderly woman in a blue smock, asks me to leave because she has to give Dad a bath. When I come back in, he is sitting on a chair with a large rubber ring on the seat, looking out through the French windows to the garden. The nurse sits by him, feeding him breakfast – pink pap from a spoon. When she leaves, I take her place at my father's side.

'Can you hear me, Daddy?'

He looks back at me with glazed eyes. We both stare out at the garden for a while. This was not what I expected when I was told I was coming home. Unsure what else to do, I just start talking. I tell him all about England. I tell him about the school. The bullies. I tell him about Martha, and Auntie Maureen and Zoe and Luke. About the food I ate. The weather. Last of all I tell him about the night I got lost and the policemen beating up the black boy. I tell him everything, and when I finish talking I feel lighter.

I can't tell if my stories have any effect on Dad. His chest gently rises and falls but I see no flicker of recognition in his eyes; I'm not sure if he is still a person inside, or just a collection of bones and flesh.

*

Mum still goes to work every day. When she gets home she spends all her time questioning Dad's nurse, checking up on the house girls, making sure Dad has eaten, checking his nappy is clean, checking his medicine bottles, talking on the phone with the doctor. She's like a tornado the way she runs around and fusses but she never just sits beside him and talks. It's like she's trying to save him, like she doesn't believe he is leaving us. But even I can tell he's going soon. It's then I realize how much Mum loves her husband.

When I'm not sitting with Dad, I explore the garden. It isn't as big as our old one, but it's full of beauty. There's a flamboyant tree in the centre of the lawn; it has bright red flowers and thick branches perfect for climbing. Over in the corner there's a pond, its surface covered with mosquito larvae. The driveway is bordered with palm trees and other plants. There's a rubber tree that leaks a thick white sap when you cut into it. The grass is spiky and hard with yellow patches where the sun has burned it to a crisp. It's nothing like the soft green English grass. This African grass is harder – it must endure a lot of punishment – and yet it survives.

CHAPTER 19

Manchester, 1990

Coming home wasn't like returning to what was familiar. Everything was different, our home, Dad, my school. The only thing that had remained the same was Mum. She was still focused completely on Dad. But I didn't resent it because when I saw my father I knew if there was ever a time he needed her, it was then. And maybe it was what she needed, to throw herself even more into my dad, to saving him; it was her last chance.

I also had to start at a new school. And although this filled me with apprehension it was at this new school that I finally stopped trying to blend in and instead let my own own colours shine.

Lagos, 1984

It's November. Another new school. This one is a private school for Nigerian children only. And once again I enter late in the school year. At least the uniform is quite pretty: a sleeveless dress with white and purple checks on it. I wear it with knee-length white socks and Bata sandals.

There's a fluttering in my stomach as I am led into the classroom but it's nowhere near as terrifying as my first day in Manchester. Even so, I don't want to be that scared little girl again. I touch the scar under my wrist from the burn Martha gave me. Then I arrange my face into a scowl and draw myself up to my full height, ready for any attack.

The teacher, Mrs Okwonkwo, introduces me to the class at their desks. 'Welcome, Lily!' they say in a chorus and I can't help but blush. The tension in my shoulders releases and I find myself smiling at them all.

Mrs Okwonkwo is wearing traditional dress – a white blouse, colourful wrapper and matching purple and yellow patterned headscarf. She has huge round glasses with purple frames that take over most of her face and magnify her eyes.

The first lesson is Maths. Mrs Okwonkwo writes a problem on the board for us to solve. Before I have copied it down into my notebook someone has answered it. How?! No one has a calculator. Mrs Okwonkwo writes another problem on the board and then holds out the chalk and motions for me to come to the front and solve it. I stand in front of the board holding the chalk in my hand and stare at the problem. My hands are sweating so much that the chalk is wet. Everyone is watching. Mrs Okwonkwo smiles and says, 'Do you need some help, dear?'

I nod. She points at a boy at the front and clicks her fingers. 'Femi, come and help your classmate.'

Femi appears at my side, takes the chalk from me and starts. Mrs Okwonkwo says, 'You can sit down, Lily.'

When Femi finishes he turns to Mrs Okwonkwo.

'Very good, Femi.'

He grins and walks back to his seat.

Have I been put in the advanced class or something? We never did anything this difficult in Manchester. I will have to let Mum know when I get home. Mrs Okwonkwo sets some more problems to get on with and then calls me to her desk. I think maybe I'm in trouble, but instead she goes through the maths with me, helping me to work through the answers.

At break, I sit in the playground eating my sandwiches – eja dadi on agege bread, sardines in tomato sauce on white bread – when a girl comes over and introduces herself as Chibu. Chibu has hair cut tight to her scalp, and full bushy eyebrows that dance on her forehead. She asks if I want to join her and her friends, and the rest of the break is a blur of clapping and hopping and singing and this new-to-me feeling of being part of a group.

The rest of the day passes quickly. At home time we all have to sit in the Assembly hall and wait for our parents or drivers to collect us. The hall is stuffy and hot with bodies and I am dizzy. When I see Peace I have to hold onto his arm to steady myself as I follow him outside to the car. When I look back the whole school is watching – but Chibu waves and I wave back, smiling.

*

149

Back at home, I go upstairs to tell Dad about my day. As I talk I look out at the garden, and when I finish, I pause and check his face. There's something in his expression today that tells me he can understand. His eyes are brighter somehow. I feel closer to being able to connect with him. My heart aches a little with the hope.

I take one of his books from the bookshelf and start reading it to him. *The Count of Monte Cristo*. As I read, a pleasant warmth flows through me . . . I think my father might finally be able to see me. Even if he can't express it in words or gestures, the sense of connection feels so pure and direct. It's all I've wanted. Now, I need to savour every moment with him . . . I know he is slipping away.

*

Chibu comes to my house one day after school. In the garden, I show her the creatures that live in the pond. She suddenly looks up at the verandah where my father is sitting.

'Who is that?' she asks.

'My father.'

'What is wrong with him?'

'He's very sick.'

She looks at me. 'Sorry.'

We decide to climb the tree. Once we're up, we sit together on a branch, swinging our feet in the air, and Chibu tells me about her last visit to her village during masquerade festival.

'Of course, I wasn't allowed to watch.' She makes a huffing noise. 'Me, a mere female!' She waves a finger around then kisses her teeth.

'But why? That's so unfair.'

'Do I know?' Chibu points at herself. 'I tell you this country is designed to favour all the boys and men.' She slaps the tree trunk with her palm.

I think about this and am slightly ashamed. I never noticed it before, or not in those terms.

'Who has to help clean the house and cook the food in my house?' Chibu jabs her finger at her chest. 'Do my brothers ever have to help at home?' Her voice is getting louder and shriller and she starts kicking the branch below us.

'Do you know what happened to me in the village?'

I shake my head.

'I was squatting down to help my grandmother cook, and I parted my legs. Well, my mother came running out of the house, slapped my face and shouted loud enough for the whole village to hear that I was a dirty girl. Can you imagine?'

'Actually, my mum shouts at me if my legs are parted too.' She's done it rarely but I want to make Chibu see that I understand. A memory of Daramola grabbing for me in the car flashes across my mind and my whole body wants to curl.

'And every time I come home from school with full marks on a test do you think I get any prizes? Does anyone congratulate me? Nooooo! In fact, the only time anyone takes any notice is if I *don't* get full marks – *then* you can bet my father will call me to his room, for a beating!'

'Oh my god!'

'Yes!' Chibu nods emphatically. 'But if my stupid brother manages to scrape a seventy or eighty per cent he's a genius!'

Chibu puffs her cheeks. 'When I grow up, I am going somewhere like America where women are treated better.'

'Then I'm going to come with you.'

Chibu laughs, gets to her feet and climbs to an even higher branch. The leaves shake as she moves. 'Does your mother beat you when you do badly?'

I shake my head.

Chibu seems shocked but it's true, my parents never beat me. In fact, I don't think I ever got into trouble for doing badly at school. They are more relaxed than most Nigerian parents. I wonder if that's a bad thing, if it means they aren't interested in my schooling, but then I wouldn't want the pressure. Especially now – I rarely get good marks at school any more. The standard here is just too high.

'Have you been to your father's village?'

'No,' I say, adding, 'but I've been to Ireland, where my mother is from.'

She nods then says, 'But why haven't you been to your father's village?'

I shrug. 'I don't know. They just never took me. I think they used to go a long time ago when my grandmother was alive.'

'How can you know your people, if you never see where you come from?'

'But I come from here, Lagos.'

'No!' Chibu's voice has raised an octave. 'Lagos is not your culture. You're an Igbo girl but you can't even speak the language.' She shakes her head.

I remember how Dad told me off for learning just a few words of Igbo, hoping to impress him.

'I don't think my dad wants me to.'

Chibu gawps at me. 'What are you talking about?' She claps her hands together. 'You must educate, eh? I will teach you.'

I nod and she smiles.

We both jump out of the tree and run to the house.

*

My new friends at school are interested in me in a different way from the children in Manchester. They like to touch my hair and ask questions about my father's tribe, can I speak Igbo, what food do we eat at home, where is my mother from and where did I go to school before. When they find out I was in England they are desperate to hear more.

I paint a nice picture of Manchester. I describe it in a way they will understand, as if life over there rolls along like an Enid Blyton book. I lie because I don't want them to be disappointed and I know it's unlikely they will ever learn the hard truth. In a way I want to protect them.

Every week, the class with the highest average in our weekly tests gets a gold star, and the class with the most stars at the end of the year wins a prize. I thought I was quite clever, but here, I realize I'm not. My maths is terrible and so is my geography so I have to spend a lot of time after school studying.

The teachers are strict and competitive but there's only one teacher I don't like. It's not just that I don't like him; I'm frightened of him. His name is Mr Oppong. He's from Ghana. The whites of his eyes are yellow and he always looks angry. He takes the class competition very seriously and when I did badly in a maths test once he stopped me in the corridor, pointed his finger and shouted, 'You let the team down and I will beat you if you do it again!'

*

There's only one bully in this school. Her name is Loretta. She's bigger than everyone else in my class. I think she is older than us and has been kept back a few years because she's not very clever. She scowls a lot and doesn't play with us at break. She stole my special pen. It's Dad's. I found it in a drawer in my parents' room and took it without asking. The pen is gold on the top half and black on the bottom and is engraved with my dad's name.

A few days later I saw her using it, and when I went to get it from her she put the pen down and stood up tall with her shoulders back. She towered over me.

'This pen is not yours. It is mine. Now get out of my way before I deck you.'

All I could do was sit back down and feel consumed by guilt.

The next day I watch Loretta closely; she writes in her notebook with the pen and then holds it to her lips when she pauses. At the end of the lesson, after the teacher leaves, I stand up, walk over and snatch the pen out of her hand. She gives me a dazed look and then her face tightens. Her chair scrapes against the ground.

'You are looking for trouble, oyibo girl, eh?' She pokes me in the chest with a finger.

'This is my father's pen. Look – it has his name on it.' I point to the inscription.

154

Loretta hisses and pushes me with both hands. I nearly lose my balance but right myself by grabbing a chair. She puts her hands on her hips. There are a few other children still packing up their things; they gather round but instead of shouting *Fight! Fight! Fight!* and clapping their hands they are shaking their heads and saying *No*.

'You can't have it.' My lips quiver as I speak and heat flushes through my body. I tighten my grip around the pen.

'Leave her alone!' a voice calls. I glare at Loretta; the whites of her eyes are bright against the dark centres. We stand like that for what seems like hours and then she lets out a long hiss, turns and picks up her things, then shoves my shoulder hard as she leaves the room. I release a long breath and put the pen in my pencil case. I will no longer be a victim.

CHAPTER 20

Manchester, 1990

My sister Sophie's wedding stands out in my memory as a happy time. It gave us something new to focus on, something hopeful. And so we all threw ourselves into the preparations. It was also a chance to observe my mother in a different context, when her thoughts were not filled with my father. On the surface it appeared she didn't approve of the marriage. She didn't think Fela was good enough for her daughter. But underlying this was a fear of losing her daughter to a man, the way my grandma had lost my mother to my father.

Lagos, 1985

Three months have passed since I came home. Christmas and New Year's Eve were very different from previous years. Maggie and Luke didn't come home. Only Sophie came on Christmas Day. We didn't eat anything special, just some yam pottage that the house girl had prepared the previous day. We didn't even bother with presents. There was a feeling of wanting to get the holiday season over and done with so it was a relief when I started back at school in January.

Sophie has finished university now. She works for a pharmaceutical company. She looks different too – her hair is relaxed and she wears it in a ponytail, and she dresses in pretty skirts and tops instead of jeans all the time like she used to. She and Fela are engaged. They live together in Yaba but she visits us every weekend. Sophie always used to seem cranky, but now, she smiles often and always talks to me when she sees me unlike in the past when she mostly ignored me. I think she is much happier than she was before and maybe Fela has something to do with that.

Mum, Sophie and I sit in the lounge one Saturday, chatting, drinking Lipton tea and eating little sponge cakes that Sophie picked up at Dallas bakery round the corner.

'How's it going with Fela?' Mum sips on her tea.

'It's going well. He is a good man, now.' Her voice comes out high and strong like a violin.

Mum wrinkles her nose. 'Living with my daughter before marrying her is not the action of a good man.'

'Oh, Mummy.' Sophie rolls her eyes.

'Living in sin is what that's called in Ireland.' Mum purses her lips.

Sophie sighs.

'Well, when is the wedding, if he's such a good man? In my day, if a girl did what you're doing she would be sent to the convent! You don't even have a ring!'

'So? *You* didn't get an engagement ring until twelve years after you were married,' replies Sophie. 'The only reason you and Daddy don't like him is because he's Yoruba. That's tribalism.' Sophie spoons sugar into her tea and stirs. The spoon makes a scraping noise in her cup.

Mum huffs. 'Your daddy would rather you married a foreigner than a Yoruba man. In my opinion, he's not your class. You shouldn't go beneath you.'

I lock eyes with Sophie. She raises her eyebrows and holds her hands in the air.

'I just don't want you to end up like me, Sophie. He'll be wanting you to have children and then you'll be completely trapped. You're better off with an expat. You don't know what's involved if you marry a Nigerian. The culture, the in-laws, uhhh! And what if he takes another wife? He can, you know – he's a Muslim.' She lifts her eyes to the ceiling.

'God, Ma! You're one to talk. Didn't you go chasing Daddy all the way from Ireland to Nigeria in the 1950s? Wasn't it even illegal to be a mixed couple then?'

Mum frowns. 'I did not! I came here on my own and worked for the British government. *He* was the one who came chasing after *me*, and I'll have you know once I got married and had children my life was over.'

We sit in stunned silence for a while, chewing cake. I try to take in what I've just heard. Eventually Sophie speaks.

'Sometimes I wonder why you ever married Daddy.'

Mum swipes crumbs off her skirt. 'Desperation. I didn't have any other better options. You children are going to be the death of me. I've had to put up with your father all these years, and now I have you giving me a nervous breakdown with your goings-on.'

My stomach tightens. Does she really feel that way about us?

'Can't you girls be independent? Men are the ruination of women! You have choices now. Opportunities. The world stretched out before you. You're educated and beautiful and you want to tie yourself up with … with … with an army officer no less!'

Sophie stands up suddenly. 'I won't listen to any more of this. I'm going to greet Daddy and then I'm leaving.'

'Fine. I hope everything is milk and honey and happy ever after.' Mum grabs another cake off the plate, shoves it in her mouth and chews it angrily, cheeks bulging and jaws moving from side to side like a cow.

This is a new side to my mother. I've noticed it since I have been back. She is more opinionated, less compliant. It's almost as though, as my father grows weaker, her personality becomes stronger. This frightens me a little.

*

For my eleventh birthday, Sophie and Fela come over with a beautiful cake made of peaches and cream. I think back to last year, how angry I was when Mum forgot my birthday, and it seems so distant now, so petty. I can't quite believe how much has happened since then.

This year, there's an extra surprise. Sophie and Fela tell us they have an announcement: they are getting married. I leap up and hug my sister (secretly hoping she'll ask me to be a bridesmaid), but when I look over at Mum, she remains stony-faced, lips a tight white line.

'You'll be leaving me for good then,' she says, eventually.

It seems nothing makes my mum happy.

Sophie laughs and gets up to hug her. I'm surprised by how tightly Mum clings to her eldest daughter, how her eyes are wet when Sophie pulls away.

'I'll still come every weekend.'

Mum nods. Sophie starts sketching out dresses and designs, and Mum and I add our own ideas – for someone who didn't want anything to do with it, Mum has some very strong ideas! The reception will be held in our front garden. After a day of birthday cake and wedding plans, the house has become lighter and brighter. I barely notice the smell of sickness that hangs in the air and sticks to my skin like wet sand.

*

There will be over a hundred guests at the wedding – small by Nigerian standards, but still a lot of work. To help with the preparations, I go shopping with Sophie at the big indoor market in Yaba, for fabric to make favours to hand out at the reception. The energy here is hectic and hot, crowded with sellers and customers shouting and joking among themselves.

Some pull their lips back over their teeth and call out to us, 'Oyinbo peppe!'

Back in the relief of Sophie's air-conditioned flat, we sit at her dining room table, filling a hundred small bags made of yellow organza with boiled sweets and tying them shut with yellow ribbon.

Maggie has been trusted with the important task of buying the dress – Sophie wants a western-style wedding gown and they're difficult to find here. Maggie has to buy it in England and bring it home for the big day. I hear Sophie on the phone to Maggie, her voice sounding urgent.

'You have the correct size, right? Ten? Shebi? You can't get this wrong!'

The call goes on for ages – not, I think, because it needs to, but because neither of them wants to be the first person to put the phone down. There is something so final about breaking that connection to the other person when they're so far away and so much can't be communicated.

*

Maggie arrives in Lagos a few days before the wedding and we all gather at Sophie's flat for an unveiling of the dress. Me, Mum, Maggie and Sophie sit on the bed and watch as Maggie pulls it out of its plastic wrapping. 'Ta dah!'

There is silence for a few seconds and then Sophie screams.

'What have you done? What is this?' She rushes forward, grabs the dress from Maggie's hands and throws it on the floor.

Mum and I glance at each other.

'How much did you pay for ... that?' says Mum. 'I gave

161

you £300, not £30! Couldn't you get something decent for your sister?'

'What's wrong with it? You said you wanted something in ivory?' Maggie's voice sounds like an out of tune piano – wobbling up and down.

'It looks like something the tinkers would wear,' says Mum. Her tongue is as sharp as a knife. Sophie wails.

'Oh come now, stop that drama. It's nicer than what I had at my wedding, I can tell you . . . Go try it on,' says Mum, waving her hand towards the dress lying on the floor.

When Mum describes her wedding day it sounds like something that was done in a rush with little thought.

Reluctantly, Sophie slips off her skirt and top. She has a nice figure, large boobs, small waist, big hips, shapely legs. If we were to stand side by side I would look like a stick insect. She steps into the dress and pulls it over her hips with Mum's help. The zipper makes a tense sound as Mum pulls it up. We all stand back to look at Sophie as she stares at her reflection in the full length mirror.

It isn't that bad, but even I know it's not a wedding dress. It's ivory, so at least Maggie got that right. The dress falls straight down to just below the knee. It isn't loose but it isn't tight either. It's shapeless. It has padded shoulders and puffy sleeves that reach Sophie's elbows, and the upper back and chest are made of lace netting.

'I look like a house girl going to church!' Sophie cries, her hazel eyes swimming in tears. Sophie is the only person I know who looks beautiful when she cries.

'What am I going to do?' Sophie slumps onto the bed with

her face in her hands. Her shiny red nail polish glints in the light.

'Maybe it's a sign,' says Mum. 'I told you, you shouldn't marry beneath you.' She looks smug, like she has been proven right.

Sophie looks up at Maggie who is still standing awkwardly in front of us. 'And what about you? What have you got to say for yourself?'

'It's beautiful, Sophie, that's why I bought it,' Maggie says, defensively.

Sophie sighs, stares at her lap and shakes her head as she mutters something to herself.

I don't think Maggie bought an ugly dress on purpose. My sisters just have very different styles. Maggie likes to wear men's shirts and jeans, or if she does wear a dress it's usually baggy and shapeless, matched with knee high boots and a denim jacket.

Sophie likes girly clothes, flowery A-line dresses, bold colours with soft lines, anything modern. I can see that Maggie was trying to imagine what Sophie would like when she bought the dress, but somehow, things had got twisted up in her imagination. There's no denying that she has made a terrible mistake.

'Come on now, pet. It's going to be fine. It's not that bad.' Mum's voice is soft and she pats Sophie on the back. 'Come on, let's have another look in the mirror.' She pulls Sophie up to her feet.

'At least I got the shoes myself.' Sophie glares at Maggie as she rifles in her wardrobe and brings out a shoebox. She uncovers it and unwraps a pair of ivory pumps with kitten heels.

Sophie stands in front of the mirror again.

'Gorgeous!' Maggie claps her hands.

'It's not that bad,' says Mum.

'It's beautiful,' I add.

'Really?' Sophie sounds doubtful.

'Yes, yes,' says Maggie emphatically.

Sophie sighs. Then she looks over at Maggie. 'You bitch.'

*

When the wedding day arrives, our house in Apapa is full of activity. Maggie also brought my dress, and thankfully at least she got that right – white on top with a fuchsia skirt that is cinched at the waist and flows out and down effortlessly. Even with my milk bottle glasses on my face, I feel quite pretty. Then I see Maggie. She's wearing a pale pink suit and a white shirt and she looks like she belongs on the cover of *Vogue*. I stare at her and wonder if she really is from this family at all. I am sorry for Sophie. There is still some time before we have to go to the registry office, so I go to Dad's room to show him my new dress. Maggie has avoided spending any time with Dad since she arrived home, only going to see him after Mum told her to. Maybe it's too difficult to see him like this.

Dad's in his chair, which has been placed on the balcony so he can watch all the goings-on when the reception starts. Our front garden has been turned into a party space with a huge white gazebo and rows of tables and chairs covered in white linen. The tables are decorated with vases of flowers cut fresh from the garden; hibiscus, roses, canna lilies.

I do a twirl for Dad.

'Do you like it?'

I see a flicker of response across his face. It only lasts a second.

'Well, there's lots of drama going on. Sophie wants to kill Maggie because of the horrible wedding dress. She's calmed down a bit but Maggie looks so beautiful and elegant today that I think Sophie's going to hit the roof when she sees her!'

There it is again. Usually his eyes are like muddy puddles but today they are bright and shiny.

'Well, I have to go now, Daddy. We're due at the registry office soon, but I'll come and see you later.' I bend down and peck him on the cheek.

Back at home after the ceremony, the guests have all arrived and are mingling in the garden when Sophie and Fela make their big entrance as husband and wife. Their limo slowly curls up the driveway, which is lined on both sides by men in fancy uniforms, Fela's colleagues from the army. Eventually Sophie and Fela emerge onto the patio, holding hands and beaming out at their guests.

Soon, the dancers and musicians come out. I sway to the drum beat which is fast and rhythmic. The dancers jump, stamp and twirl white handkerchiefs in the air as they move. After the performance, the DJ starts playing a cool mix of soul classics and the food is brought out. I fill my belly with jollof rice, okra stew and moy moy.

I go upstairs to check on Dad. He's still sitting in the chair, watching the party below. The gazebo blocks his view but it's just possible to make out Mum, Sophie, Fela and his parents at the high table. I haven't been able to think about all the ways he would have loved to join in the celebrations – making a speech, dancing with his daughters, playing the proud father and generous host. I tell him all about the ceremony, about Maggie looking so beautiful, about the guests, the food, the dancing. But this time, when I look at his eyes, I see hollowness again. The only sign of his presence is a gentle quiver at his lips, as though he is whispering to himself. I sigh and sit back in my chair, take his hand and hold it in mine.

CHAPTER 21

Manchester, 1990

My father's passing didn't affect me in the way it affected the rest of the family. My mother and siblings were all bereft, they cried constantly and comforted each other. I watched all this outpouring of emotion and found that I was numb. It was as though I was no longer in my body, but instead, observing everything from a distance. I didn't particularly feel sad, and this frustrated me greatly because I thought it meant I was a bad daughter. Back then I didn't know how to process the feelings of grief. Grief was a wound inside me that, at first, I was able to ignore but as time passed it grew bigger and more tender until I had to face it.

Lagos, 1985

Dad has stopped sitting in his chair during the day. Instead he stays in bed and his nurses turn him every few hours to relieve the pressure on his bedsores. When I get home from school he's usually asleep. Mum is more irritable these days, lashing out at the staff and at Sophie when she comes to visit.

I sit on the sofa with my legs tucked under me, reading. Caroline, our house girl, dusts a chest of drawers. Suddenly, I hear Mum racing down the stairs, and when she enters, her face is flushed and shiny. I put my book down and sit up.

'Why didn't you give the Master his pap?' she says to Caroline. 'I will not have the Master being mistreated. I won't have it. He deserves to have what he likes.' A vein on Mum's temple pulses under her skin like a swollen river.

Caroline frowns. 'But I gave am, madam.'

She can't look my mother in the eye. Even I can tell she's lying.

Mum reaches for the first object she can lay her hands on – a silver tray – holds it up high and thwacks it down hard on Caroline's head. The sound makes me wince. Stunned, Caroline rubs her forehead and stares at Mum with her mouth open.

'Mum,' I say, 'what are you doing . . . ?'

She's scaring me. Her face is so twisted with rage I hardly recognize her. Her mouth twitches, her body shakes, her eyes are small points of grey. Caroline and I instinctively back away.

As though completely exhausted Mum slumps into a chair. 'Get out of my sight,' she says, quietly.

Caroline drops to her knees. Her skirt rises up to reveal thick calves and the yellow soles of her feet. She bows her head to the floor and cries loudly.

'Please, madam. A beg, sorry oh.'

Caroline lifts herself up and presses her hands together, begging for forgiveness as she backs away towards the kitchen.

Mum pushes herself out of the armchair and makes her way back upstairs, leaning on the banisters with each slow step, as though all her strength has been sapped away.

Caroline stands in the kitchen, looking terrified, tears still streaming down her face. I used to eat my meals at the kitchen table after school, even though Mum says it isn't appropriate, and Caroline kept me company, telling me all about her life growing up in the village. She was sent to Lagos as a young girl to work in a big house. The Madam of that house was a wicked woman who would beat her so badly that eventually Caroline ran away. This made me think of how I felt in Manchester, how I wanted to run away too. She told me how she lived on the streets for a long time before she found another job as a house girl to an old widow. She was happy there for many years until the widow died. As she told me these stories about her life she worked away, chopping, peeling, stirring, pounding yam.

Now pain flares under my left eye, as though someone has pierced it with a hot needle. Mum never treats the staff badly. She sometimes speaks harshly if they miss something or don't do things to her liking, but she has never hit them. There is something terribly wrong.

I go upstairs and pause outside my parents' room. I can hear my mum, talking, sobbing. I open the door a crack. Dad is lying on his side facing her, she is sitting next to him. I quietly close the door again and slip into my room. My whole body is cold even though it's baking hot. I lie down, grab my old blankie and press its rolly bits under my nails. Something is shifting in my world again. I put on my Walkman and blast the music loud so that I can't think.

*

Dad is getting weaker. His every sound is like something being scraped against a piece of rough wood. Is this death? The body folding in on itself, slowly breaking down from the inside out?

Once I saw a dead lizard in the garden. I watched it over a period of weeks. At first flies covered its body. They were then replaced with maggots. As they began to eat it away, it also started to decompose, to rot, to smell, to become something else no longer a lizard. Is this happening to Dad? And what's on the other side – burning flames or paradise as I was taught in church? Has Dad been a good person? I worry that he might end up in hell because of The Incident.

Dad sleeps. He seems to be shrinking. He can't eat and has a needle stuck in his arm which feeds him liquids from a bag. It makes me cringe when I see the needle poking under his skin, the flecks of dried blood around it. Mum and Sophie take turns sitting with him. When my sister sits with him, she weeps quietly and shakes her head from side to side. Dad makes soft noises and at one point he raises a hand and rests it on her arm. I notice as he gets weaker he is more aware of us, he is able to communicate through touch and using his eyes.

'You have to live, Daddy,' she says to him. 'You can't leave us now, it's too soon. I haven't had children yet. I want them to meet you.'

My father looks away and seems to fall asleep.

Eventually Sophie leaves me alone with him. He opens his eyes and looks at me. I hold his hand and notice how cold and light it is. His body is so thin it looks like it could float away, but his eyes, they are large and burn with such intensity that I believe he is trying to tell me something. But what is it he wants me to know? I place my ear next to his mouth to see if he can whisper it to me but all I hear is the crackle in his lungs as he breathes.

*

As the days pass, I press my fear down into my stomach. Something tells me that this time is precious and shouldn't be wasted. When he's awake he looks frightened, his eyes search the room for Mum, as though she is what he needs to stay alive. I watch them for hours while she holds his hand and talks with a soft voice, reading him poems by Christina Rossetti and Emily Dickinson and passages from a book by a French author named Emile Zola. This surprises me because I've never seen my father read anything other than the newspapers. Did he once love books the way I do? What else don't I know about him?

At one point she leans in close and says, 'Do you remember when we met? All those years ago when you were a student. Those trips we had in my car out to the Wicklow mountains, the picnics on the grass. How beautiful it was.'

Tonight, she tells me I have to sleep by myself. I tell her I don't want to. The idea of sleeping alone in that big room terrifies me. Her face hardens and her lips press into a line. I get the message and go to my room.

Later, I hear voices in the hall. I get up and open my door and see two men – one of them is Dad's doctor. They both look serious, but as they pass my door, the doctor sees me and smiles gently.

'Go back to bed, dear,' he says.

I close the door, crawl into the bed and cover myself with the sheet. I can't listen to my Walkman or read and I certainly can't sleep so I just lie there, holding my breath, paralysed by a feeling I don't understand.

After what seems like hours, Sophie comes. She sits beside me on my bed and reaches for my hand. Her eyes and nose are red and her lips are swollen.

'Daddy has passed.'

The words hang in the air. The only sensation is the absence of feeling all over my body.

Sophie stares at me as tears run down her face. It is just weeks since her wedding. Why can't I cry like Sophie, like a good daughter? I'm ashamed.

'I have to go now to Mummy. Lily, do you want to see . . . ?'

I shake my head. 'It's OK.' She clicks the door closed.

I hug my knees and wait for the sad feelings to come but they don't. There is only a sense of numbness and that numbness floating in space.

*

The funeral happens on a Sunday in April. Maggie and Luke come home from England. Mum's brother, my uncle Malachy, comes from America and Dad's relatives also arrive, my auntie Ada and two cousins, sisters in their thirties called Nkechi and Ife. I've never met them before. Dad's sister looks just like him. She has the exact same eyes, nose and high forehead so that every time I see her face, I see my father staring back. The house is full to bursting.

On the morning of the funeral four men carry Dad's coffin into the lounge and set it down on a table that has been brought in for that purpose. The other furniture has been moved out and plastic chairs set up all around the walls. One of the men opens the casket 'for the viewing'. My heart gives a lurch.

People take turns to go up and say goodbye to my father. His relatives sing a song in Igbo. The sad melody and their pained voices make me burn.

I wait my turn in a corner, quietly, almost timidly. I want to see Daddy but I can't bear the thought of an audience or any kind of pressure to move along. Only when everyone else has paid their respects do I approach the coffin. The first thing I notice is that he has grey spikes of hair on his chin. Each and every morning, right up until the end, someone came in to shave him. How is it possible his beard has grown? Beneath the bristles, his skin is smooth and waxy. There is cotton wool stuffed into his nose, ears and mouth. I think about him leaking away.

He is wearing one of his grey suits and a white shirt and burgundy tie. There is a strong chemical smell. I want to stay by his side for as long as possible. I pull up a plastic chair and sit and look, hard, so that every line and curve of his face is seared into my mind. And then, a sickness reaches my stomach and a twisting pain in my chest which gets worse.

What happens next is like watching myself from afar.

Someone calls my name and I become aware of activity in the room around me. The scraping of chairs across marble, people talking. I see myself getting into the car. We go to a huge church with lots of people. The family is sitting on the first two rows.

I see Luke stand at the altar to read from a paper in his hand, so serious and grown up in his black suit. Other people come up and talk about Dad and then the priest reads from the Bible. I am next to Mum who is silently crying. Her lips tremble. She is wearing a black dress and clutching her leather handbag. She holds a rosary between her thumb and forefinger, rubbing the beads with her thumb, over and over, and I wonder if the movement soothes her like my blankie does for me.

I still haven't cried.

I'm ashamed, bow my head and hope no one notices what a terrible daughter I am. I pick at a scab on my knee and think about Dad. The bad times. The terror. Then of the last, peaceful months we had together. But still, I can't cry.

After the service we go to the cemetery. As we walk deeper into the grounds, a heavy silence descends, as though someone has thrown a thick blanket over the day. There is a strong smell of earth and something else and I think it might be death.

Men lower my dad's coffin into the ground with ropes.

Auntie Ada screams and shouts in Igbo, she slaps her head

then lurches forward. Her oldest daughter, my cousin Nkechi, holds her back and whispers something in her ear. Frightened, I grab Mum's hand. The noise of my auntie's keening gets under my skin. I want her to stop.

We each take turns to pick up a handful of dirt and throw it onto the coffin. The dirt lands with a thud. The sound of an ending.

The gravediggers pick up their shovels to do the rest. Soil against the wood.

Afterwards, walking back to the car, I ask Mum about Auntie Ada's outburst. I know he was her brother, but the wildness of her reaction felt so out of place.

'She wanted Daddy to be buried back in their village, with a traditional Igbo ceremony – not here, near us. She thinks his soul won't be at rest.'

'Will it?'

Mum pauses. 'Of course it will, Lily. Your daddy wanted to be close to his family, close to us. He's resting in peace now.' She reaches down and strokes my cheek. Her touch is like silk running over my skin and I savour it.

Back at home, the formalities keep going around me; and as I stand in a corner of the lounge, watching, I begin to feel as if I am a ghost. A man in a white kaftan, blue baggy trousers, a skullcap and black leather slippers stands up and pours schnapps on the ground to make a libation. He breaks a kola nut and passes it round. The house girls place large pots of food and pitchers of drinks onto the dining room table. Someone puts music on. People mill around the dining room and parlour. I stand leaning on the drinks cabinet and feel like the chameleon I so longed to be in Manchester. A man I don't know knocks into me as he reaches to open the drinks cabinet; he blinks with confusion as if shocked to see someone standing where he was certain no one had been before. He apologizes and grabs a bottle of gin.

At some point I lay my body down on my bed upstairs and gaze up at the ceiling, wondering what being at rest really means.

*

By the following evening all the relatives have left. It's just us, me, Mum, Luke, Maggie, Sophie and Fela. Luke went out tonight and didn't come home till late – he stumbled through the front door at 2 a.m. We are waiting for him.

'Show some respect!' shouts Sophie. 'What are you doing going out drinking and drugging at a time like this!'

'You're a disgrace!' says Mum.

Luke pushes past me and runs up the stairs. Mum and Sophie follow, still shouting. Then I hear a scream and a thud. I run up the stairs to find Luke, cradling his fist. There is a dent in the bathroom door.

'You're always all against me!'

Luke lets out a wail that is so full of pain we all freeze in shock. His sobs are powerful and loud, coming from somewhere deep inside him. He collapses to the ground and we rush to him. Sophie kneels and wraps her arms around him and Mum holds them both. Everyone is crying.

'It's OK. It's OK. It's OK. We love you,' says Sophie. She rocks Luke back and forth. Mum holds tight and lets herself be swayed by their movement. I don't know what to do so I join in and hold onto Mum. We all remain like that until Maggie emerges from my room, headphones on her head, a confused sleepy look on her face, and asks, 'What's going on?'

CHAPTER 22

Manchester, 1990

After my father's death I thought my mother would finally be all mine. That her attention would move straight on to me. But it wasn't like that. The loss changed her. She was still angry, but then she had periods when she would retreat inwards. I was so used to seeing her as a ball of energy it was jarring when she was still and quiet, with tears running down her face. In those moments she looked helpless and I resented that, even in death, my father claimed all of my mother's love.

Lagos, 1985

The following week Maggie and Luke go back to England, Mum goes back to work and I go back to school.

I still haven't cried.

When I get home from school that first day, I go upstairs to tell Dad all about my day. I am halfway down the hall before I remember he's no longer here and a tightness wraps around my heart.

Later that evening, when Mum's back from work, she takes the gin bottle out of the drinks cabinet and pours till her glass is quarter full. Then she goes to the kitchen and tops it up with tonic water and a couple of ice cubes.

I tell her about my day. She listens closely and the more she drinks the more she starts to laugh and make jokes. By the time she's finished her third glass, her cheeks are pink and her lips form into easy smiles and her eyes grow heavy. She falls asleep in the armchair and I have to wake her up and lead her to bed.

In the morning Mum is back to being angry. She yells at Peace on the drive from Apapa to Victoria Island: for not servicing the car properly, for not buying the diesel for the generator, for not bringing her back enough change from some shopping errand she sent him on. Peace keeps quiet through her long tirade; she calls him lazy and ungrateful and incompetent and I wonder how he is able to just sit there and take it. I put on my Walkman to block out the sound of her voice.

*

179

That night, when she reaches to open the drinks cabinet, I get there first, holding the door shut. My mother looks to me, mouth slightly open, eyes flashing. I swallow the ball of fear in my throat.

'No,' I say, with a firmness that surprises me.

'What?'

'You've been drinking too much.'

It looks like she's about to shout but then she closes her mouth and nods.

'OK, Lily. OK.'

*

Mum and I now sleep in the end room. Neither of us can stand to be in the master bedroom – it's still Dad's room.

*

It's Saturday afternoon and Mum is sitting at the dining room table dealing with paperwork.

'Be a good girl now and get me the red folder in the master bedroom, pet. It's in the first drawer of the dressing table.'

I go, even though I am afraid. Upstairs, I hesitate for several moments before I can muster the courage to turn the key and open the door. The first thing to greet me is the sour, sweet smell of Dad in sickness. I don't know how I even enter but I force myself forward, towards the dressing table. I sit down on the velvety stool in front of the large mirror and rummage through the drawer. Once I find what I need, I glance up at the mirror and see my father's reflection staring at me.

Dad is sitting upright on the end of the bed. He is wearing

180

his burgundy pyjama top and bottoms and his brown leather slippers and he smells of Old Spice. He smiles and reaches out his hand in my direction. I scream and race out, locking the door behind me.

'I saw him! He's upstairs in the bed!'

She looks up at me in shock. 'What do you mean?'

'Dad! I saw him upstairs.'

'No, you didn't, you didn't see anything, pet. It's all right.' But her voice is thin and high.

My whole body is shaking and my heart is a bird trying to escape from the cage of my body.

'I saw him, Mum, please go and look.'

'OK, if it will make you feel better.' She plants her hands on the dining room table and stands up and climbs the stairs. I follow close behind.

When we get to the room, she looks at me briefly and then unlocks the door. She pushes it open and switches on the light. The same smell hits me. She goes and stands in the middle of the room and waves her hands around.

'See. Nothing here.'

I look around and there's no one there. As we leave, Mum closes the door a little too quickly and it bangs shut.

I know what I saw. I think that, when we die, everything that makes us who we are leaves our body and so we become spirits. If a spirit misses their family too much they come and haunt them.

That's what my father is doing. Haunting us.

*

School is a distraction from my thoughts but then it's the summer holidays and the days stretch out before me like an infinite road. With no one to talk to and nothing to do, I read until my eyes grow so tired they twitch.

I watch videos of American films; *St Elmo's Fire*, *The Goonies*, *Weird Science*. I rent *Witness* from the video shop and when I see Danny Glover the hairs on the back of my neck stand up because he looks so much like my father. I have to turn it off. Then I watch *The Legend of Billie Jean*, which makes me want to be brave and strong and beautiful like Helen Slater.

Then I find a film called *Frances* in the video shop; it has a photo of a pretty blonde woman on the front, the reviews say it's riveting. I watch it alone one afternoon, completely transfixed. It's the life story of the 1930s actress Frances Farmer. I watched as Frances is put in a mental hospital and given electric shock treatment. I think of my father in the hospital and wonder did he have to go through the same treatment, was he frightened like Frances? My eyes fill with tears as I watch Frances suffer at the hands of the nurses in the hospital, who rape and beat her, hose her down with cold water. It strikes me how completely vulnerable she is, under the control of others, how she has no power over anything once she is inside. At least my father had my mother to watch over him.

I lose myself in these films and now, when I bang, I replay the scenes in my mind until I am somehow in them. Time passes for me like this.

I am trapped in the house. I no longer have any interest in exploring the garden, I'm too old to make it a magical fairyland, and I don't like the way the new gardener's eyes follow me everywhere. He reminds me of Daramola so I stay away from him.

There is nowhere for me to go, no shops like in Manchester, no Arndale Centre, no park to hang out in, not even a corner shop for sweets. The only interesting place is the market but I can't go there by myself, and besides I hate the noise, the heat, the crowds pushing against me, the confusion of trying to make it through the narrow paths. But the worst thing about the market is the smell of rotting fruit and vegetables; that odour stays with me long after I have left. I want to go to the Rec Club in Ikoyi and swim but Mum says I can't go on my own and she is too tired to take me after work.

So, instead, I spend my time obsessing about death.

I want to know what it feels like. I go to my old bedroom – the room I never sleep in any more – lie down on the bed, close my eyes and hold my breath for as long as I can. I try blotting out my thoughts, keeping a black, blank screen behind my eyelids. Soon, though, my lungs burn as if they're going to explode and my inner vision is a kaleidoscope of brightly flashing lights.

I don't give up. I try again, this time pinching my nose shut and clamping my hand over my mouth. My eyes water and I can't stay still so I get up and walk around the room in circles, noticing the white desk, a pile of books, my pink pencil case, the red wardrobes, the red curtains. Then there's darkness the colour of blood and suddenly I am on the floor, the room spinning and my whole body shaking.

Then I breathe. I breathe and I breathe. Pure relief. The simple act of inhaling and exhaling has never in my life felt so necessary or pleasurable.

Next I try the bath. Usually we have bucket baths, because water is so scarce we have to ration it carefully, but for once there is enough water so I can fill the tub just enough to submerge my head. Once I am under, I close my eyes and listen to the water sloshing against the side. As it becomes more difficult to hold my breath I try to concentrate on staying still. I see bright sparks and a tingling feeling patters across my scalp. My heart pounds loudly against my temples. Then as though someone has flicked a switch, complete stillness, darkness, nothingness, as though I have dissolved into tiny particles. Then, strong hands wrap around each arm and pull me out of the water. I gasp and splutter and wipe my eyes. When I look around there is no one there.

After that I give up trying to experience death.

*

When Mum comes home from work she tells me all about the drama in her office. Another Irish Nigerwife has started working there. According to my mother, the woman is the Devil incarnate.

'Do you know she smashed my cup on purpose?' Mum chews on a buttered cream cracker. 'And now she's accused the cleaner Mercy of stealing photocopying paper. I don't believe she stole it. I think Margaret framed her. She's a very unhappy woman, that Mrs Afia.'

'What did Mercy do?'

'She denied it of course. Got down on her knees and begged Mr Nolan.'

A vision of Caroline comes back to me, prostrate on the ground begging my mother.

Mum gives a short laugh and says, 'Peace and the company driver offered to have her dealt with.'

I gasp. 'What?'

'Pious is from Calabar. Your daddy told me people from Calabar poison their enemies so he would know how to do it so no one would ever know.'

'Mama! You aren't serious?'

'What? No! Of course not!' But I notice a look in Mum's eyes, a hesitation, as though it's something she has thought about.

Mum shakes her head and lets out a noise that sounds like *Ha!* Some crumbs are stuck to her lips. I wish she would brush them away. Looking at them suddenly makes me sick.

'Dr Odeyemi called me to find out how I was.' Mum's face changes, smooths out like a piece of silk. 'He's a real saint that man. He even told me I should remarry.' She cackles – like a goose calling to its mate.

'Would you remarry?' I see a faceless black man in our life. I can't imagine her with someone white. My back tenses at the thought.

'Are you de craze? You think I would put up with another man? I gave thirty years to one, that's more than enough.'

CHAPTER 23

Manchester, 1990

I used to think constantly changing schools was a disadvantage, that it didn't give me the chance to make long-term friends. Instead I was needy and possessive and latched onto anyone that would have me, always dreading the inevitable separation that came with moving on. It was destabilizing having to reinvent myself every few years, trying to find a place to fit in. I know that's probably why I am so shy and self-conscious, but there's another side to this: perhaps it's made me more adaptable, more resilient and able to survive in new places. I've met people who grew up in the same place all their lives and they are just as insecure and shy as I am. So maybe it's more that the way other people treat you influences how you feel about yourself.

My mother is always saying I shouldn't care so much what other people think of me. But is it really possible to live in the world and not care?

Lagos, 1985

As the summer draws to an end all conversations turn to my schooling. There are various private foreign schools, the Japanese one, the German, the French, the Italian ones, but I don't speak any of those languages. There doesn't seem to be a suitable private English-speaking school here according to Mum and Sophie, and no British secondary school.

I think Mum is keen to send me abroad. I overheard her talking to Uncle Malachy about it after Dad's funeral.

'You need to think of her future, how she'll adapt for university. I'm guessing she'll be going abroad eventually,' he said.

Uncle Malachy is an investment banker in San Francisco and I suppose Lagos must have seemed very strange to him. While he was here, he picked me up from school one day. During the car ride home, he asked me questions about what I wanted to be when I grew up, that kind of thing. I noticed how his light blue eyes widened as he listened to me speaking. When we got home, I ran to the garden to join Peace's children who were climbing the tree. We all shrieked as we swung from the boughs. I saw Uncle Malachy standing watching us, open mouthed and a handkerchief clutched in his hand, as if he'd never seen children behaving so badly.

Sophie is the first one to suggest the American school.

'But can you afford it? It's the most expensive school in the country.'

Mum pauses. 'I can manage. We still have the rents coming in and the dividends from the companies. It will be a squeeze, though. We'll have to be careful.' She looks at me and I study my knees.

'But it would be worth it. I've heard it's such a good school,' says Sophie. My sister seems to be getting prettier every day. She was one of the models for her company's calendar. She brought the calendar for us to see. There were lots of pretty girls smiling at the camera for each month, but my sister was the prettiest. She has such large eyes; they are hazel and they give her a sweet, gentle look.

I try not to get too excited about the American school but I can't help myself – my life is spent watching American movies and TV series, listening to American music, and I feel ready for the adventure. Everything there will be bigger and better because it's American.

In bed at night I fantasize about how I'll make lots of new friends and be part of a popular girls' clique. When I wake up in the morning I have an incredible feeling of happiness.

*

The American school is in one of the richest neighbourhoods in Lagos. There is a long driveway up to the entrance. On my first visit to meet the principal, Peace drops us there. The American flag billows in the wind. A huge square playground is surrounded by the U-shaped school building. The principal, Mr Adams, is tall with wispy blond hair.

In his office, Mr Adams and my mother talk for a while. Every so often he glances in my direction and smiles. His office is nicely air-conditioned. The walls are lined with portraits of famous Americans: President Kennedy, Martin Luther King, Billie Holiday. There is a big poster called 'Fall in Virginia'. It's nothing like autumn in Manchester. The shelves are full of books, some textbooks but also novels: *To Kill a Mockingbird*, *Catch-22*, *Crime and Punishment*, *Things Fall Apart*. On the desk is a family photo – his wife and two children I guess.

Eventually Mr Adams turns to me. 'Your mom tells me you love books. Who are your favourite authors?'

For a moment I stare at my bare knees which look particularly knobbly. Mum nudges me with her elbow.

'I like Thomas Hardy, Charles Dickens and J.R.R. Tolkien.' My reading tastes have progressed a lot. After I discovered how fake Enid Blyton's version of England was, I felt betrayed. I don't mention the other novels I've been secretly reading – by Stephen King, Danielle Steele, Sydney Sheldon, Taylor Caldwell, D.H. Lawrence and A.J. Cronin.

'Very nice. You'll find we have a big library here that you can use. So what are your favourite subjects at school?'

'English . . .' I look at Mum, ' . . . and Science.' This is the right answer. She told me Dad wanted one of us to be a doctor like him, and since Sophie is a lawyer, Maggie is studying law and Luke is in the British army, now it'll have to be me.

'Good, we have an *excellent* Science teacher. Mr Richardson. All the students love him. Here is some information and your timetable. You'll be going into the sixth grade.' He hands me a pile of papers and a small booklet about the school. His accent makes me feel like he's a character in a movie.

'It's been great to meet you, Lily, and I look forward to having you here.' He reaches out to shake Mum's hand and then he takes mine and grins.

*

When I found out you don't have to wear a school uniform I was initially excited, but I hadn't realized how difficult it would be to choose what to wear instead. I need to look cool, but not stand out. For the first day of school, I choose a mid-length dress, with a geometric pattern in white with blue cutting across it diagonally. It has a slit up each side. As Peace joins the queue of cars in the driveway I feel a sudden need to go to the toilet. As we near the entrance, I see groups of students chatting and laughing together, with their backpacks and jeans and t-shirts, and instantly I know my dress is all wrong.

'Good luck!' Peace smiles and nods.

'Thank you.' I hesitate as long as I can before hopping out of the car.

I keep my head down, avoiding eye contact as I race to find the toilet. I'm standing at the basin when the bell clangs for class. I rush out of the bathroom so I'm not the last to arrive – I don't want to be stared at.

When I find the classroom, I join a line of students outside, waiting to be ushered in by the teacher. Eventually I reach the front. 'Welcome to sixth grade,' she says. 'Lily, is it? I'm Mrs Smith.' She's got long red hair and bright green eyes. She smiles and shows me a set of perfect white teeth. I take an empty seat near the back of the class.

There's a girl sitting in front of me with long blonde hair reaching all the way down to her waist. She keeps flicking it behind her and it lands on my desk. This irritates me greatly. As I watch the curtain of her hair move, I have an incredible urge to grab a pair of scissors and cut it all off.

Mum told me to look out for a girl in my class named Roisin – her boss Mr Nolan's daughter. I hope she isn't the girl sitting in front of me. Mr Nolan is Irish too and Mum said I should be friendly to her. This automatically makes me dislike her. When the bell goes for recess – as they call breaktime here – I hear someone call her name. Roisin has shoulder-length reddish blonde hair, blue eyes and freckles. When she passes me, I smile and say hello. She flashes me one of those smiles that look like insults because they happen so fast and are quickly followed by a scowl. I guess she doesn't want to be seen chatting with her dad's employee's daughter.

Outside in the big central courtyard, everyone breaks off into groups and I find myself standing alone. Two teenage boys are standing on a balcony above the yard, looking down right at me. One looks like a typical American – pale skin, blonde hair, blue eyes and muscular build; the other is smaller, thinner, with dark hair – he looks Lebanese. They are talking and laughing as they watch me, probably making fun of my stupid dress. I wish I could figure out how to be a chameleon here – I'll have to learn fast.

I have a strange sense of being in a movie. The sound of

American accents is all around me. It's been a long time since I was surrounded by so many expatriates in Lagos.

'They are junior high kids,' says a girl with an American accent and over-relaxed hair. She's wearing a t-shirt and shorts and a pair of white trainers. 'I'm Ifeoma and this is Ngozie.' She introduces the girl next to her, with long reddish brown hair tied into a ponytail – I can't tell if it's a weave or relaxed.

'I'm Lily. Thanks . . . are they still looking at me?'

They exchange a look and I realize with horror I've spoken with a strong Nigerian accent. Ifeoma sniggers.

'Ignore them,' says Ngozie. 'That's Bassim and Rino. It's because you're a new girl.'

'What school were you in before?' Ifeoma raises her eyebrows as she speaks.

'Green Hill.'

She closes her eyes and nods as though everything has become clear. 'Do you live in Ikoyi?' she asks.

'No, I live in Apapa.'

Ifeoma nudges Ngozie and they quickly move away from me as though I've just farted. I make a mental note to mimic the way everyone else is talking.

I didn't know living in Apapa was a bad thing until now. It seems everyone here lives in Ikoyi or Victoria Island. I do know what they mean, though. They are the best areas. Everything that's fun and interesting is there, the Rec Club, restaurants, shops, and all the expatriates apart from the Syrians and Lebanese who mainly live in Apapa. I want to tell them that I used to live in a big house in Ikoyi when my family was rich but I keep my mouth shut.

The students here come from all over the world. There are a few Brits, Israelis, Lebanese, Pakistanis, Indians. One or two Chinese. Swedes, Danes and Dutch. Brazilians and Venezuelans. You can count the Nigerians on one hand. I haven't met any actual Americans so far.

In our classroom there's a big map on the wall with lots of pins of various colours representing all the different countries in our class. When I'm asked to add mine, I decide to add two, for Nigeria and Ireland.

Every week someone does a presentation about their country and culture and they bring in traditional food for us to try, but beneath the surface there is a kind of hierarchy that exists. There are cool countries to come from and uncool countries. America is the coolest of all, then Canada, Britain, followed by any European country and Israel which seems to be equal in coolness to Europe. Next comes South America, and the Arab countries. At the bottom of the cool list are India, Pakistan and anywhere in Africa. There aren't any Australians as far as I know so I'm not sure where they would fit. Probably with America.

No one has explained this hierarchy to me; it's made obvious by the way everyone behaves. It's the other Nigerian kids, like Ngozie and Ijeoma, who annoy me the most. They put on strong American accents, saying things like *Awesome!* and *Rad!* too loudly, and at lunchtimes they strut around in the latest American-style clothes and eat peanut butter and jelly sandwiches. It's like they have ironed out their culture along with their hairdos.

It's not fair to say all the Nigerian kids are like this, but

193

Ngozie and Ijeoma are and I am definitely not cool enough for them. Bitches. I thought they would want to be my friend because I'm half-caste.

*

Despite being lonely for these first few weeks, the school has been fun. I really like the American way of learning. The teachers are very nice and treat us with a respect that I'm not used to. There's no such thing as beating students like in Green Hill or any kind of corporal punishment. They actually ask our opinions and instead of giving us long lists of things to memorize, we have discussions and do fun games and activities.

The only problem I have at school is my lack of friends. Penetrating the white girl cliques is nearly impossible. It's not that they dislike me exactly – I'm just invisible to them. I wanted to be a chameleon, but now I at least want to be interesting enough for them to notice me. I know if I was American or European or Israeli they would flock around me like I was a superstar.

I've taken to spending recess in a corner with a book. It's worked before. Usually when I'm focused on reading, I can ignore the anxiety about having nobody to hang out with, but today I am distracted and feeling miserable.

'Hello, I'm Hilda.'

I can't place the accent. I look up to see a white girl wearing an old-fashioned blue dress, with an embroidered pattern on the chest.

'Hi, I'm Lily. Where are you from?'

'I'm from Rhodesia. Oh no! It's called Zimbabwe now.'

'Where's that?'

'It's in Southern Africa.'

White Africans? I sit forward with interest. 'How come you're here?'

'My dad had a farm back home but we had to leave it when the government changed.' She looks sad when she says this and I realize she's lost something important too.

Hilda wears a brace on her teeth. She's bony, like me, and her brown hair is cut short.

'Do they hurt? Your braces.'

She nods and quickly covers her mouth with her hand, then shrugs her shoulders. 'But my mum said it will be worth it in the future so I can put up with it.'

'What's Zimbabwe like?'

Hilda closes her eyes and smiles. 'It's beautiful. The most beautiful country in Africa. Our farm had lots of different animals. We had cows, goats and horses.'

'I'd like to go there.'

'What about you?' Hilda studies me curiously.

'I'm from here in Lagos. My mum is Irish and my dad is . . . I mean was . . . Nigerian.' I glance at Hilda. There is something in her face that makes her look older than she is. I like that about her. 'He died a few months ago.' The air stills. Saying it aloud gives it a new kind of power, makes it more real.

Hilda puts her hand around my shoulder. 'I'm so sorry. You poor girl.' She pulls me close and wraps her arms around me and although I am uncomfortable I also realize that I am crying into her shoulder.

From that moment on, we are best friends.

CHAPTER 24

Manchester, 1990

Once I made friends with Hilda I settled more easily into the American school. While my school life was improving, life outside school was deteriorating. The situation in the country had grown turbulent and difficult after a military coup. There were more armed robberies, and instead of just leaving with what they found, they were killing people. There was anxiety in the air, it filled your lungs with a gritty feeling that hurt your chest. Walking through the gates of the American school was an escape to another country – a much safer, happier country.

Lagos, 1985

There has been a coup.

Mum and I are in our bedroom. In the barracks behind our house, the soldiers are hollering and shooting, letting off rounds indiscriminately.

'Get under your bed!' Mum shouts. She crouches and watches me scramble under my bed before she tries to crawl under hers. I hold my palms over my ears and squeeze my eyes tight as the gunshots explode in the air. There's the crashing sound of a window breaking. After a few minutes they stop. All we can hear is the neighbour's dogs barking. I slowly crawl out and see Mum's bum, sticking out from under the bed, too big to fit underneath it. The laughter starts as a giggle and then erupts into loud guffaws. It's a kind of hysteria – part relief, part terror. It comes from the pit of my belly and I can't stop. Eventually Mum scrambles out on her hands and knees and stares at me for a few moments, eyes hooded, mouth turned down.

'Lily?'

'You ... looked so funny, bum in the air ... nose to the ground.' I hiccup and before I know it the tears of laughter turn into deep sobs, drawn from a well in my belly. I cling to Mum and we hold each other tight until my sobs have turned to sighs. Later we walk around the house to check the damage. There is a bullet hole in the window by the stairs.

After that, the army set up checkpoints on the roads. The soldiers often stop us and search our car as though we are hiding someone. One morning they stop our car outside the American school. They point their machine guns at Peace's head as he opens the boot. They don't ask me to get out but one of the soldiers stands next to the window and stares at me. He fondles his gun and smiles. He has red eyes and a fat, hand-rolled cigarette hanging from his mouth.

I am only a little anxious because the idea of soldiers harming me, a half-caste girl, seems impossible. In the past I have seen soldiers pull people out of their cars, but it's only men who are targeted.

Once they finish their search, one of the soldiers shoves Peace's back with the tip of his gun. Peace turns around to face him, eyeing the soldier slowly from head to toe with a smirk. I hold my breath. Peace draws himself up straighter and juts out his jaw. The soldier raises his gun and points it at Peace's chest. The moment stretches out like a long piece of string.

'Oya now, leave dem!' A soldier waves at Peace to move along. Peace kisses his teeth as he turns his back. The soldier holding the gun continues watching us as we drive on.

'You shouldn't have done that,' I say.

He doesn't answer but I see that he is gripping the steering wheel tightly and when he drops me at the entrance he doesn't say his customary goodbye, just drives off.

When I get into class I sit with Hilda and tell her about the soldiers, leaving out the part about Peace.

'They did the same to me,' she says and pulls at a piece of her hair.

Several others add their own accounts.

'They pointed a gun at my driver,' says Eva.

'Me too,' says Eyal.

'Did they open your boot?' asks Dev.

It's the first time any of those kids have spoken to me, or even acknowledged my existence.

'There were gunshots outside my house. A bullet went through a window,' I say.

Eyal's green eyes grow wide and he stares at me as though noticing me for the first time. He's Israeli and very good-looking.

*

The student protests start a few weeks later. We are driving back from Victoria Island when we get caught in the riots. Before we leave Mum's office, Peace tells her to sit in the front. He hands us each a small palm branch which symbolizes our support for the protest.

We are stopped on Carter Bridge, crossing into Apapa. Men and boys run amok in the road, wielding bats and machetes. I try to swallow but my mouth is dry and sour. Two of the men wave down the car in front of us. They pull the driver out and start beating him. Next comes the passenger sitting in the back. A woman. One of the men grabs her by the arm and throws her on the ground. He starts to beat her. She lies with her hands up trying to protect herself. On the other side of the car, there is a man with a machete. He has the driver crouching on the floor in front of him. The driver is on his knees, begging. The man with the machete raises it high above his head.

'Lily! Cover your eyes!' Mum screams and reaches back to grab my arm.

I put my head down and hold a hand over my eyes. There

is a thump as a man jumps on the hood. The car shakes with his weight.

'What do we do?' Mum's voice frightens me.

'We give him money. They are touts, not students.' Peace shakes his head.

Mum reaches into her bag and pulls out a wad of naira notes. Another man comes to the driver's side of the car and knocks at the window with his bat. The man on the hood is smiling; he pulls out a machete and waves it. Peace winds down the window and hands the money to one of the men. They leave us. As we drive past the car in front, I close my eyes. I don't want to know what has happened to the driver and his Madam.

*

Everyday life becomes more difficult after the riots. It's hard to get things. Medicine, supplies and any kind of foreign food. A few times there is even a petrol shortage. Peace queued for twelve hours at the station one time. Nigeria is one of the largest producers of oil in the world and Mum say's it a disgrace – she says the oil all goes to foreign companies and since Nigeria doesn't have the infrastructure to produce its own petrol we have to buy it from abroad.

Death is everywhere, almost incidental to daily life. Every day on the way to school we drive past a dead body. The man's body has been there for weeks. Peace says he has probably been knocked down trying to cross the expressway. One day as we pass I see a huge bird feeding on his carcass.

Mum is having trouble at work again. She has a new manager, Mr Kelly, who is also Irish. He bullies her every day. With

Mrs Afia as his willing sidekick, he makes her run in circles with no reward, punishing her with extra work. She has to stay later and later at the office, and Mr Kelly doesn't care that it isn't safe to cross into Apapa from Victoria Island after dark. When Mum does eventually get home she tells me everything and I'm left with an impotent rage.

Mum isn't home yet. She rang at about 6 p.m. and said she would be late. I spent the whole evening with my eyes glued to the window. It's 11 p.m. now. My head fills with visions of armed gangs laying nails across the road to stop the car. Peace swerving. The gang dragging Mum and Peace out ... and worse.

When Mum finally arrives home I run outside. Her face is blotchy with red patches and her eyes are glassy with exhaustion. She comes inside, sits on her armchair and places her hands on her lap. She shakes her head and whispers something.

'What?' I lean closer.

'I don't know what we are going to do. I can't give up this job. I have to stay no matter what that man does to me. I'll never get another job here.'

'How can he be allowed to do this?'

'I'm a local employee and a Nigerwife. I have no rights.'

'Can't you complain to Mr Nolan?'

Mum makes a sharp noise. 'That coward! He's afraid of Kelly – *and* Mrs Afia.' Mum weeps. I put my arms around her and rub her back. 'I don't know what to do, Lily. I just don't know what to do.'

I run to the phone and call Sophie. Even though it's late, she picks up on the third ring. I am so incoherent that Sophie tells me to give the phone to Mum.

'I don't know what I'm going to do. It's unbearable ... But I can't leave. I need the foreign exchange. How will we live? How will I pay the school fees? How will I pay for Maggie in university? What am I to do?'

I can hear Sophie's voice on the other end of the phone. Her tone is soothing and calm. I realize how much pressure Mum is under and it strikes me just how alone she is, a widow with no one to support her, her family halfway round the world and rarely in touch, Maggie and Luke back in England. Sophie and I are all she has.

I go to the freezer, plop two ice cubes into a glass, fill it with gin and hand it to Mum. She's grateful and takes a long sip. As she continues drinking and listening to Sophie, I watch her face grow calm; she even manages to laugh at something Sophie says. After a while she says her goodbyes and puts the phone down. She places the empty glass on the side table and holds out her arms. I go to her.

'I'm sorry I frightened you, Lily. I just had a really bad day. What would I do without you and Sophie, eh? My good girls.'

*

Mrs Afia's youngest daughter dies the following week. She is killed in a car accident – she dies at the hospital, on the operating table. There was a power cut. She was my age.

I go with Mum to the funeral. We stop first at the house. Mrs Afia lives in an underdeveloped part of Lagos I've never been to before called Oworonshoki. I begin to wonder if this is why she hates my mother.

Peace lets us out in front of Mrs Afia's building. The gutter by the block of flats runs thick with human waste and other things. We have to cross it on a wobbly wooden plank. When we find her flat, the windows are protected with metal bars and the walls outside are peeling and covered with green mould. The front door is open but there is a bead curtain hanging across the entrance that clicks as we enter the dark stuffy room beyond. I've met Mrs Afia a couple of times. She has short dark hair and a bullish look about her with a stocky round body and a square-shaped face. But now she looks like a ghost, dressed in black, holding a tissue to her red nose. Her usually red face is grey and the skin has dropped as though she has lost weight. Her red-rimmed eyes are confused as she stares at the closed coffin on a table next to her. Mum goes to her and takes her hand.

'I'm so sorry.'

Mrs Afia looks frightened as she gazes at my mother; after a few minutes she pulls her hand away and returns her eyes to the coffin.

At the cemetery we follow the procession to the grave. The pall bearers carry the small coffin on their shoulders. My heart gives a lurch as one of the men – the girl's father – seems to lose his balance. The gravediggers take over now, wrapping rope around the coffin and lifting it and lowering it slowly into the ground. Several of the mourners wail and wave their hands in the air. They stamp their feet and sing traditional songs. The family gathers close. Mrs Afia's two remaining daughters, both teenagers, hold onto their mother and cry softly.

The priest reads out his sermon. Mrs Afia can barely stay on her feet – only her husband's strength holds her up. I study the grave and a hot shame courses through me. I wished God would punish Mrs Afia. I wished it and now I wish I could undo every evil thought. But I know death doesn't work like that.

*

As though in punishment for my sin a gang of armed robbers tries to break into our house. Mum hears them shouting at Musa, the gateman, ordering him to open up. He refuses. Mum picks up the phone to call the police but there's no dialling tone.

'Jesus Christ this country!' she screams.

Suddenly there's a gunshot outside. My blood chills through my body. Without wanting to, I peer at the scene from our bedroom window. Musa is still standing, thank god, trying to calm things down. Soon, a police jeep arrives and four policemen jump out. One of the neighbours must have called. There is more shouting, more shots fired, then silence.

I never found out exactly what happened but things settle down. Musa is safe, everyone has moved on, Mum's okay and asleep. But I can't stop thinking what would have happened if they had got further. If they'd found me. I wonder what a gunshot feels like. I wonder if I would die quickly or slowly. I wonder if I would be with Dad again.

CHAPTER 25

Manchester, 1990

My mother was struggling in those years. She had lost her husband of thirty years and was a single parent living in a country where day to day life was often very difficult. She forced herself to work at a job she hated so she would have enough money to support us. And to top it off she was a Nigerwife widow. She was neither an expatriate nor a local. This meant little or no support from the outside world. The other Nigerwives tried to help, they called on us frequently, sent care packages, offered to do things, but my mother often rejected their help, preferring to retreat into herself and view the outside world as the enemy. Every day was a battle. She was either shouting at everyone or she sat on her bed, held her head in her hands and cried. When I saw her like this my skin burned and my heart twisted in anguish.

I resented her back then. All I knew was that yet again I wasn't the centre of her universe and it made me madder than it did before. There was no one standing between us any more. So why couldn't she finally be happy? Why wasn't I enough?

Lagos, 1985

Life with Mum has become even more difficult. It's more than having to listen to her tell me about the office and all her anxieties about money and the future. It's that she never wants to do anything fun.

Every Monday our teacher asks us what we did at the weekend. Nearly everyone has something exciting to report, a trip to the beach at Tarkwa Bay, or a party. I lie and say I went to the beach or out with my sister, to avoid telling the boring truth.

My weekends go like this. On Saturday mornings me and Mum go to the supermarket, then the Lebanese store, then to the video shop to return the tapes we've watched and get new ones. After that she spends a few hours at the dining table doing paperwork. She calls Peace in and gives him a list of tasks for the following week. After she sorts out all the household business she places her elbows on the table, presses her fingers into her temples and narrows her eyes.

'I have a migraine coming on.'

This is the signal it's time for her to go and lie down, where she stays for the rest of the day. On Sunday she doesn't even come out of the bedroom. Instead she takes all her meals in bed like an invalid, leaving me to watch films on my own and fantasize about the life I could be living if I were like one of the popular girls on the telly.

In the past Mum used to socialize with all her Nigerwife friends. They used to have weekly meetings in a church hall and sometimes I would go along. Other times she would host tea parties at our house in Ikoyi and they'd talk about their lives in Nigeria and the challenges they faced, from their husbands' families and even from their own. I guess they all formed a close bond, but since Dad died my mother barely ever sees them.

Today, though, one of them comes to visit.

It's Sunday afternoon. We are in our room, me lying on my bed reading, Mum listening to the BBC World Service. We hear the scrape of the metal gates as a car drives in and a horn beeps outside. Mum rushes to look out of the curtains which are always kept drawn on Sundays.

'Don't open the door whatever you do. And switch off the air conditioning, so she doesn't know we're here.'

'Who is it, Ma?'

When she doesn't answer, I peek out; it's a German woman I recognize from our days in Ikoyi. I don't understand why Mum is playing this charade with her friend – Musa will have told her we're here.

A few minutes later the front doorbell rings. Mum puts her finger to her lips and gives me a wild look. She gets back into bed, pulls the covers up to her chin and stares at me defiantly. She reaches for her handbag and, as I knew she would, takes out her tablets. I have noticed she is taking more and more of these tablets throughout the day. The bell continues to ring and the sound goes through me. Mum turns on her side, puts both hands on her cheek and slowly closes her eyes. Finally the woman gives up trying. A door opens and closes, the engine starts, the car drives off. I turn back to Mum. She has put an eye mask on over her eyes and is lying on her back, a faint smile on her face.

'Put the air conditioner back on,' she says.

Lagos, 1986

Hilda left in the New Year. Her family has moved to England, leaving a gaping hole in my life. Hilda is the only one who understood me. She was also a gateway to the other kids. I doubt the other kids will want to hang out with me when we go back for the new term.

I hate the way everything keeps changing. There is nothing to grab on to, to steady me. Sometimes it's like I am sitting on the shore of a river, watching people, places, things flow past me. All I have is myself.

*

I've decided to have a party for my twelfth birthday, and to my surprise Mum says I can. I make the invitations by hand. Everyone in my class says they will come and some of the girls have said they'll sleep over.

As the day approaches I get more nervous. Sophie drops off a cake and the catered food arrives, jollof rice, okra stew, egusi stew, rice and yam. The house girl fries enough plantain to feed twenty people. Paper plates and plastic knives and forks are put on the dining table, paper cups for drinking the glass bottles of Fanta, Coke and Sprite and red party napkins decorated with balloons.

I put on the dress I wore to Sophie's wedding. Then Mum and I sit in the lounge and wait. The time for the start of the party comes and goes. We put on a video to distract ourselves. An old episode of *Top of the Pops*. Madonna is singing 'Holiday'.

'Did you put the correct time on the invitations?' Mum stares at the TV as she speaks.

'Of course I did,' I reply with irritation.

An hour passes and my stomach starts to rumble.

'Maybe you should have something to eat,' says Mum.

'I don't feel like it.' My belly is tied up in knots.

After another hour there is a beep at the gate. A car drives in. It's Dipti. Now she jumps out smiling with her overnight bag in her hand. She is the kind of girl that fits in with everyone. Unlike me, she moves through the world easily. In school she is always friendly towards me.

Mum welcomes her and then disappears and leaves us to the awkward silence. We have some food but I am too humiliated to enjoy it. I expected Dipti to say something about being the only one here but she doesn't. She turns to me with her bright open face and asks, 'What shall we do?'

I put on *The Breakfast Club*, my favourite movie, and eventually I realize I'm actually having a good time. After the film we play Monopoly and Connect 4. I put on a video of *Soul Train* and we copy the dancers and laugh until we cry. When Mum comes down, she lights the twelve candles on my cake and she and Dipti sing happy birthday. Dipti tells me to make a wish and as I blow the flames out I quietly wish that she will be my new best friend.

At school on Monday, I'm still ashamed that none of the others bothered to turn up and I am sure they'll all be laughing about it. In the end no one says anything or even looks at me funny. What hurts me most is Dipti – although she chats to me for a little bit, perfectly polite and sweet, she doesn't invite me to join her and her friends at recess and it's clear she's never going to be the close companion I found in Hilda.

*

I've been at the American school for over a year when I start seventh grade, junior high. Over the summer it seems like all the girls have sprouted breasts and have waists and they share stories about shaving their legs for the first time. These changes haven't happened to me.

It's not just physical changes. Most talk centres around boys, and recess is spent in cliques rather than playing in the square. The girls in their cliques behave like they love each other, they are always hugging and holding hands, but there is intense competition between them – you can see it when a popular boy walks past or talks to them. They all vie for his attention. I observe all this from a distance, wishing that I was part of it all.

I hover on the peripheries, making no impression on anyone. I think back to my time in Manchester. Back then, I wanted to be invisible, like a chameleon, so no one would hurt me; but in the American school I long to be noticed, for them all to see how nice I am, for everyone to like me.

It's not that I don't try. Sometimes, when I'm feeling brave, I try to get attention by being the funny girl in class. I do great imitations of Michael Jackson, kicking my leg high, grabbing my crotch and flicking back my head then screaming, 'Owww!'

It always attracts a crowd, everyone enjoying the show, but as I do the same moves over and over, my audience grows bored and their eyes glaze over and they move away.

*

A new girl has joined the class. Her name is Razia and she's from Pakistan. She's funny and witty and has a clever way of describing people, making fun of the way they walk or speak. After a while, we begin to hang out. We bond over the fact that neither of us is cool enough for the popular crowd. Razia doesn't seem to care. We settle into a friendly routine after a few weeks. We aren't soul mates or anything, but she is fun to be around and it's better than spending recess by myself.

Things start to go awry when I notice Razia becoming close to another girl in my class, Meera. At first, they just pair up sometimes and whisper and giggle – I might be a bit jealous but I'm not too worried because Razia and I still hang out at recess.

Then one day we are sitting on the stairs eating our lunch when Razia says, 'Why do you always work with Yael? She's a bimbo.'

I look up at her with surprise. Yael is a classmate – she's Israeli, and one of the best-dressed girls in our year. Everyone loves her and I am flattered that she likes pairing with me.

'She doesn't even like you,' continues Razia, 'she's just using you to help her to get ahead.' I am not sure what to say. Yael isn't even an outside lessons friend.

'She isn't a bimbo. She's quite clever actually. Anyway, you and Meera work together and I don't hassle you about it,' I say defensively.

Razia stamps her foot at a nearby lizard and her face flashes with a meanness that shocks me. 'I don't see why you don't work with *me* in class. I bet Yael talks about you behind your back.'

I let out a breath. I don't want to stop working with Yael. Being her partner slightly improves my standing in the unwritten hierarchy, and anyway she must really love working with me because she could pair with anyone she wanted.

But I worry about Razia and our argument for the rest of the afternoon. She makes a big point of walking arm in arm with Meera between classes, talking secretively and giggling in a way that makes me nervous.

Thoughts whirl around my head like seagulls fighting for food and at home time I decide to confront her. I find her standing with Meera at the lockers and tap her on the shoulder.

'What is wrong, Razia? Why are you angry with me?'

She turns to me, scowling – reminding me of Gladys, back in Manchester.

'Don't touch me,' she says.

'What's wrong?' I repeat, trying to hide the panic in my voice.

'I don't talk to losers, that's what's wrong,' says Razia. 'Go away and leave us alone.' And then she uses the N word and I am stunned. It's like being slapped across the face. I gasp for a moment and try to recover.

'Piss off!' I shout, and then I add a word I learnt in Manchester, a word I've never said before, and as soon as the word leaves my lips, a feeling of wanting to shed my own skin comes over me. Razia stares at me gobsmacked. Meera also looks shocked and puts her hand to her mouth. I grab my books and hurry down the stairs and out to the car park, still unable to believe what I've just said.

Peace is waiting. I climb into the car and burst into tears.

'Ah ah! Whatin happen? Why you dey cry like dis?' asks Peace. He turns and stares at me, eyes wide.

But I can't talk. Peace drives, heading to Mum's office. In the back seat, I weep more quietly. When we get to Mum's office I wait in the heat of the stifling car, hyperventilating while he goes to find her. A few minutes later Mum comes out, a worried expression on her face. When she sees me, she raises her hand to her collarbone.

'My god! What happened?' She opens the car door and slides in next to me. 'Peace, go and get some cold water from inside.' She rubs my back for a few minutes without saying anything. The pressure of her hand is soothing until eventually I calm down enough to speak.

'It's my friend Razia. She dumped me for Meera and then she called me the N word.'

Mum turns bright red and I recognize that look from when she hit Caroline.

'What? How? I am going there right this minute to complain.'

'Noooooo!' I wail. 'I'll be humiliated. You can't say anything.' Tears stream down my face again. 'I did something bad afterwards . . .'

And then I tell her, sobbing like a baby.

'OK, OK, calm down, Lily. Let's go home, pet. I'll leave early, I'll say you are ill. You're such a delicate little flower.' She pats my back and smiles. 'You are too trusting, Lily, you wear your heart on your sleeve. You need to toughen up and realize you can't trust anyone, not even your best friends. Once they think they've got one up on you – that's it.'

Mum's words make me more depressed.

We are stuck in traffic for two hours and by the time we get home, my chest feels like someone has stamped on it several times. I go straight to bed and fall into a disturbed sleep.

The next morning, my eyes are still red and swollen and my face is puffy. My heart still aches. I really don't want to go to school, but Mum makes me.

When Razia and Meera arrive, joined at the hip as always, I try to ignore them but the more I tell myself to look away the more I want to know what they are doing. The tension is unbearable. The feeling that there are two people in the world who hate me makes me want to disappear. It makes all the bad things I believe about myself seem true.

The rest of the day is spent like this. I go from lesson to lesson feeling strange in my body. Then close to home time Meera comes up to me, alone.

She glances over her shoulder and then says in a low voice, 'I'm sorry about what Razia said.' Then she rushes away.

I want to cry with gratitude but I hold the tears back.

*

As the weeks pass, things move on. At first I thought I would never recover, but time ticks and it gets less and less painful until one day I can think about Razia without wanting to cry, without feeling anxious or ashamed, without feeling much of anything at all.

CHAPTER 26

Manchester, 1990

The transition from being a child to a teenager was not smooth for me. My body betrayed me from the inside out. I had never been completely comfortable in my own skin but when I turned thirteen this sensation grew much stronger. With the sudden physical changes in my body came self-hatred. And for a time, I forgot who I was, where I came from and lost that inner resolve to never let anyone make me feel less than them.

Lagos, 1987

When I turn thirteen, my body changes in ways that shock me. First, the sweating I've always suffered with becomes a thousand times worse. It spreads from my palms to my armpits and my crotch and, mortifyingly, it often seeps through my clothes in those areas, showing up in dark patches. The sweating makes me nervous and so I sweat even more. I will never be able to hold a boy's hand, not that any boy would want to hold hands with a girl as ugly as me.

While other girls at school seem to blossom, my body certainly isn't an unfurling flower or an emerging butterfly. In addition to the sweating, thick hairs have sprouted on my legs, crotch and underarms. I spend a whole day studying all the girls in my class and realize only me, Ngozie and Ifeoma have hairy legs – all the other girls have perfectly smooth skin. That night, I go home and tell Mum I need a razor.

'What would you need a razor for?'

'To shave my legs.'

Mum giggles. 'Don't be so silly, sure I never shaved my legs in my life!'

'Well, you don't have thick hairs like me. See.' I hold up my leg and point. 'I look like a gorilla.'

She studies my leg and makes a small noise. 'In my day, girls didn't shave their legs.'

'Mum.'

'All right, all right. I see the times are changing. Just mind you don't cut yourself.'

The house girl is sent to the market and when she gets back I rush upstairs to the bathroom and lock the door. I sit on the toilet seat, rest my foot on the side of the tub, and spray shaving foam all over my leg. I sprinkle on a few drops of water, smooth the fluffy foam up and down my shin, and then draw the blade against the hair. Smooth skin appears like magic. When I finish, a few cuts have appeared, but otherwise it feels . . . amazing! I go to show Mum.

'Touch the skin!' I say.

She runs a finger down my leg.

'Oh, *that is* smooth.' She smiles. 'Make sure you put some moisturizer on.'

But when I wake up the next morning, I run my finger up my leg and touch sharp sandpaper bristles. My heart sinks. The hair is already growing back.

I get up and force myself to stand naked in front of the mirror. The only part of me that hasn't changed are my breasts – they remain as flat as two pancakes. I don't recognize the person staring back at me in the glass, and burst into tears.

Ugly, unlovable new me.

The morning I get my period, it's nothing like I had imagined. First, the shock of the stained bedsheet and confessing to Mum, who says congratulations but is obviously upset at the thought. She can't look directly at me.

'We'll need to get you some pads,' she says brusquely, going to the bathroom and returning with a wad of cotton wool. 'Use this for now, that's what I had to do. Stuff it in your panties.'

I have more questions but her face closes like a door. She gets ready for work.

The day at school is a minefield. My period is heavy and I am terrified the blood will leak onto my shorts and everyone will see. Also, there are no bins inside the toilet cubicles so I have to wrap the soiled cotton wool in loo paper and wait until the bathroom's clear so I can shove it in one of the baskets by the sinks. I worry someone will know the bundle is mine. Eventually I become so nervous that I start carrying them in my pockets and then stuff them in my school bag to dispose of at home.

That's not even the worst of it. That comes later, at the end of the day. Pain, like someone is twisting my insides. It is so intense I have to vomit. Then it hits my bowels and I have diarrhoea. Mum pulls her tablets from her handbag.

'Take two every four hours.'

After a week, I am exhausted and weak. I can't believe I will have to go through this every month for the rest of my life.

'It's the curse,' says Mum, sagely. 'All women have to bear it.'

*

The terror of junior high is Bobby. He isn't popular so he tries to get attention by acting like an obnoxious brat.

At home time I am by my locker, putting my books into my bag, when Bobby suddenly appears by my side. He stares at me with a look of disgust and then turns to everyone and says loudly, 'God, she's so ugly it hurts my eyes to look at her.'

He opens his mouth wide in a pained grimace. Some people look away, others laugh, some smile and shake their heads. I turn and hide inside my locker door, my face and scalp burning with shame. I grab my bag and run, managing to make it to the safety of the car before I let go and wail. Peace is used to my crying fits after school and lets out a sigh.

'Why you let these people make your life so difficult? Ehhh? Why you no listen to your mother? What she dey say ee true now.'

At dinnertime I tell Mum about Bobby and what he said. Sophie is visiting on her way back from the office and she rubs my back as I work myself up into a hysterical frenzy.

'Jesus, God, get her some brandy!' says Mum. She points to the drinks cabinet. 'There beside that bottle of gin. Yes.'

Mum pulls me up by my shoulders.

'Come on, drink.'

I swallow the foul liquid down.

'Breathe.' Sophie takes my glass and puts it on the table. 'That boy's a nasty idiot. Ignore him, pet.'

'Don't let them see you're afraid. Next time he says anything, kick him in his privates,' says Mum with a nod.

'She can't do that, Mum,' says Sophie. Mum ignores her.

'You're too sweet and gentle, Lily. You need to toughen up and be strong. Stand up to them.'

Great. I'm ugly, I'm weak and I'm a disappointment to my mother.

CHAPTER 27

Manchester, 1990

It was funny how all my emotions were so intense during that time. I became sensitive to things that I hadn't noticed before, like the sunset, the taste of egusi stew, film soundtracks, books I read. I moved from sadness to intense joy in a matter of seconds. I would say this period of my life was the one when I felt most alive.

Lagos, 1987

In the middle of the school year, a new boy arrives at school. His name is Michael and he's from America. He looks like he just stepped out of a music video with a bouncing way of walking as though he is listening to hip hop. His hair is cut short around the sides and the front bit is floppy and dyed blond. He wears baggy shorts, rock band t-shirts and Converse trainers. He's got an earring in one ear and he's the coolest person who has ever been in our school. He's in ninth grade. Within a few weeks he starts going out with Astrid, another ninth grader. Astrid is Swedish and gorgeous.

The more I learn about Michael the more I start to wonder if being cool isn't so much about where you come from but how you act. Michael also lives in Apapa, a fact that I thought made me a virtual pariah when I first arrived. Not only does he live in Apapa, he's my neighbour – his house is three doors down from mine.

Michael is the best-looking boy I've ever seen and I am convinced that we are meant to be together. There are just too many things we've got in common for it to be all coincidences.

1. Michael is also half-caste.
2. Michael's mother is Irish (American).
3. Michael lives in Apapa.
4. Michael goes to the same school as me.
5. Michael's cousin is my new best friend.

Michael's cousin is a girl called Esther. She is in seventh grade with me and, like me, is often the butt of Bobby's bullying. He picks on her because she looks different to everyone else. She has thin, short legs, one longer than the other, which makes her walk with a limp; one hand is withered and wasted. She struggles to keep up in class and needs a little extra help from the teacher. Despite Esther's limp, we play volleyball together, not trying to beat each other – we're both pretty bad at sports – but just enjoying the games. She's easy to be around. I like her a lot.

Esther must have told Michael I live near him because, to my utter shock, one day Astrid actually speaks to me. She asks if I can give her a lift to Michael's. The fact she is suddenly aware of my existence is almost too much to bear.

I haven't paid much attention to Astrid until now – her social status is so far removed from my own that she is more like a film star to me than a flesh and blood person I pass every day in the school corridors. But as she speaks to me I am struck by her; it's not just her beauty, it's the way she looks directly at me, the way she smiles openly and makes me feel as if I am worth talking to.

I immediately agree to giving her a lift and even manage to find the courage to suggest she has lunch at my house with Esther first.

'That sounds fantastic!' replies Astrid with a wide smile. She claps her hands in excitement and something flutters in my chest.

I am completely elated for the rest of the day and every time I spot Astrid she gives me a little wave and a smile. Yael notices and asks if I know her. When I tell her that I do, and that furthermore she's coming to my house for lunch tomorrow, she looks completely puzzled, clearly trying to work out why Astrid would hang out with me.

*

I've instructed the house girl Victoria to make fish and chips for lunch – it was either that or hamburgers and it's silly how much I've agonized over what we should have. In the end, the fish and chips are a hit. Astrid's never eaten that kind of freshwater fish before.

I think I might float with joy.

After lunch we go into the lounge to watch a film. Astrid settles on the sofa with Esther, pulls her feet under her and gives a little sigh.

'Your cousin is the most gorgeous guy I've ever met,' she says. Esther giggles.

'He's really good-looking,' I say.

I choose *Weird Science*, put the video in the machine and settle back as close as possible to Astrid without sitting on her.

'He's like you, such beautiful skin,' she says, reaching towards me and running her fingers up my arm. Every single hair on my arm stands to attention at her touch.

I smile, hold up my forearm against hers, which is tanned golden brown, and say, 'We're almost the same colour.' I quickly take my arm away when I remember the hairs.

After the film we go up to my room and I show Astrid all my clothes. I have a nice collection now, as Maggie and Luke send me clothes from England through various family friends who travel back and forth to the UK.

'You can borrow anything you want,' I say.

I sit on a chair and watch as Astrid and Esther look through my wardrobe. Astrid pulls out a grey and yellow striped t-shirt and a black maxi skirt.

'Can I try these on?' she asks, raising her eyebrows.

I nod and to my surprise she strips off right there and then. Her body is perfect, smooth and slender with a waist that goes in and a flat stomach. I have to force my eyes to move away from her – in the end, I stare at my River Phoenix poster.

'What do you think?' Astrid does a twirl.

She looks at herself in the mirror, turns this way and then that, pulls her hair up into a ponytail then lets it flop around her shoulders. I wonder what it must be like to walk through the world in her body.

Astrid looks at her red Swatch watch and gasps, 'Oh, I have to go! I'm late!'

'Of course,' I say, 'we'll walk over with you.'

When we've dropped her off at Michael's, me and Esther link arms and stroll back along the street.

'She's really nice, isn't she?' says Esther.

*

The library has been transformed into a disco for the school dance. Me and Esther sit by the wall, watching Astrid and Michael move around the floor. They are so perfectly coordinated. I love them both.

Then the most extraordinary thing happens. Astrid comes over and pulls us both up to dance. Cyndi Lauper's 'Girls Just Wanna Have Fun' is playing. Astrid holds my hand and swings it back and forth as we dance. My palms are sweaty but Astrid doesn't seem to mind at all.

When the song is over, I go and sit back down. Yael runs and sits beside me. I think she finally realizes that I am someone of worth.

CHAPTER 28

Manchester, 1990

The friendship I had with Esther and Astrid increased my confidence. Even though Astrid left at the end of ninth grade I wasn't devastated. I found that I was someone of value and instead of clinging to one person I floated from group to group. I was still at war with my body, my looks, but something was blossoming inside me, not quite a flower but something else. I was even able to accept my mother's emotional absence and understand that I would never be able to make her happy. This thought was a shard of ice lodged in my chest and although the pain was always there, I was able to distract myself from it because I was happy at school.

Lagos, 1987

It's eighth grade and my social standing at school is more fluid than it used to be: sometimes I hang out with Meera and Dipti at lunch, sometimes I spend recess with Esther and a new girl, Judy, who is American. Other times I just go to the library and read. I don't care as much about not having a clique or a best friend, happy now to drift between groups.

Also, I have a new crush – Jason. At the moment, Meera and I both hate Yael because she has stolen him from us. We talk about it over lunch.

'I don't see what's so great about her,' I say.

'Yeah, I mean she's got such small eyes, and those tiny rabbit teeth.'

'I just don't know what he sees in her.'

'She's got a sexy body.'

Yael does have an amazing figure, curvy in all the right places, and she wears clothes that hug her nicely, tank tops, tight shorts, miniskirts. She always manages to look effortlessly glamorous and coordinated.

'Do you think they've done it?' I say.

Meera bursts out laughing. 'I don't think so, Yael keeps saying she won't . . . but she'll do everything else.'

I pause for a moment. 'Like what?'

Meera shrugs her shoulders, 'Are you asking me? I haven't got a clue.'

I sigh loudly. 'Why can't Jason like me!'

'Join the queue.'

We burst out laughing as the bell goes. I stand up and pull Meera to her feet and we head to our next class.

*

Jason is best friends with a boy called Segun and a Greek boy called Nick. They call themselves the Three Amigos after their favourite film and they are the coolest boys in the grade. Segun is kind of an anomaly because although he is Nigerian he is considered cool. Girls don't drool over him in the same way, though – they'd never dare break the unwritten code. Segun is cute, he has a mischievous face, but he isn't very tall. He makes up for that with an absolute confidence that doesn't come across as arrogance. There is something special about him that draws you towards him. He has the brightest eyes I've ever seen – they seem to become shinier when he looks my way and the dimples in his cheeks stand out more. Segun has shown me that the hierarchy of coolness can be dismantled and smashed to pieces if you believe in yourself – don't try to change who you are to please other people. This doesn't come naturally to me, but I'm getting better at it, I think. Sometimes I chat with Segun and Nick after class about music or movies. Nick's really a bit of a goof-ball, he's easy to be around. It's surprising how comfortable I am when I'm around them. I'm still shy and self-conscious a lot of the time, but yeah, I'm feeling better about myself these days.

I'm talking to Nick and Segun about a River Phoenix film I've just seen when Jason walks into the classroom and comes over to us.

'What are you guys doing in here? Come and shoot some hoops with me.'

They all bump fists in greeting.

'Amigo, it's too hot for shooting hoops,' says Segun and laughs. He shakes his head, gives me a knowing look and says, 'Americans, eh!'

I giggle.

Jason sits down reluctantly. The atmosphere has changed and I don't want to speak in case I say something stupid. The boys talk among themselves. Segun tries to include me in the conversation from time to time but Jason obviously doesn't want me there.

'Well, guess see you later,' I say, making to leave.

'You going?' says Segun, his mouth drooping slightly.

'Yeah, I need to see Mr Barry about something.'

'OK, see you!' he nods.

'Bye,' says Nick.

Jason gives me a side-eye. He clearly hates me.

*

At the next school dance, something happens. I stand by the banisters, where two boys were staring down at me on my first day of school. I remember the moment – me in my silly dress, feeling terrified – and all of a sudden I realize how far I've come since then. Suddenly, I hear a noise and look up – it's Bassim, a ninth grader, the boy who was staring at me on my first day. He's Lebanese and he's looking at me, with narrow green eyes.

'You have no idea, do you? You're so . . . ' He slams his palm on the banister and it vibrates. He leans forward and I think I let out a gasp as the penny drops: Bassim likes me. Perhaps he has liked me for a while.

We just stand there in silence, eye to eye, until a friend calls him.

That's all that happens – hardly anything really. But it's such a thrill!

'What are you grinning at?' says Meera as she comes over.

'Oh, nothing.' I shake my head not wanting to share anything, for fear I'll make a fool of myself.

'Did you see me dancing with Asif?' She smiles proudly.

'Yes, I did, are you two . . . ' I raise an eyebrow.

'No way!' She flaps a hand at me and throws her head back with laughter.

And even though no one asked me to dance tonight, when I go to bed I can't sleep with the excitement. I stay up late imagining me and Bassim as boyfriend and girlfriend until eventually I drift off.

*

Life has definitely improved. I'm invited to parties on weekends, I go to the dances, Mum even lets me meet my friends at the club some weekends and we hang out by the pool all day.

Bassim hasn't asked me out or even said anything since that night at the dance, but I see him staring at me more.

I think I look a bit better than I did a year ago. I'm still too tall and skinny and flat-chested but everyone says I wear cool clothes and I'm quite good at putting makeup on when I go to parties. A bit of kohl around the eyes, a pop of blusher, some pink lipstick. I look quite natural, but when Yael does

230

her makeup she ends up going overboard and looking like a witch.

So, yes, I'm happier than I was a year ago. But still, deep down, I sense the darkness is still there in my core, and behind my smile I live with the secret fear that it would take nothing for me to become that lost girl all over again.

CHAPTER 29

Manchester, 1990

As a child I was terrified of my father because of his behaviour. But when I got older and met my cousin Chike who also had what I learnt was schizophrenia I saw my father wasn't the demon I had built him up to be.

I was scared of Chike – he was the image of my father and he had the same mannerisms. It was like seeing a ghost. But as I observed Chike it was clear he was very ill and that illness rested somewhere in his mind. This hit me hard because it meant perhaps I had been unfair to my father, maybe there was no need for me to run away from home and reject him the way I did. If I had stayed, maybe I would have understood him better. I wonder if my father was aware how frightened I was of him and how this made him feel.

These regrets lie heavy in my heart but there isn't anything I can do to change the past. I just have to accept that's what happened. At least now I understand my father, I know he was a good man and that he loved his family. It wasn't his fault he had an illness that affected his behaviour.

I was angry with my mother – for making me decide my fate when I didn't have all the information. And anyway I was far too young to make such a big decision. It was hard knowing my mother wasn't perfect, that she had faults and she could also make bad decisions. I think we become grown-ups when we figure out that our parents are just people, doing the best they can while struggling to deal with what life throws at them.

Lagos, 1988

It's Saturday morning. I am still half asleep, but when I open my eye a slit I see Mum sitting on her bed, fully dressed, looking into her compact mirror and putting on lipstick.

'Where are you going?'

'Upsadaisy you, go and get ready. We are going to see Mrs Abiola, leaving in half an hour.'

It's been years since my mum's gone on a social visit.

'Really?'

'Yes, Mrs Abiola has found a Nigerwife who needs our help – the husband kicked her out and she's been living on the streets. Mrs Abiola took her in.'

I can't imagine a white woman living on the streets of Lagos.

I know Mrs Abiola from the wives' meetings I used to tag along to with Mum. She's American, from Texas. I remember seeing her and her husband at Daddy's funeral. When we arrive, a house girl leads us into the lounge. Mrs Abiola is wearing a purple and white tie dye kaftan. She holds out her arms and sweeps my mother into a hug.

'Cara. It's good of you to come.'

'Betty,' Mum says.

Mrs Abiola motions to a black leather sofa and then looks at me.

'How are you?'

'Fine, thank you, auntie.' The leather squeaks as I sit down.

A girl with long braids and a pretty face comes into the room. She must be about my age.

'This is my daughter Bisi. Bisi, why don't you show Lily your room?'

I follow Bisi until we reach a door bearing a clear sign:

THIS IS BISI'S ROOM
ENTER WITH CAUTION

Inside, the walls are covered in posters of pop stars, but what I'm mostly awed by is her bookshelves packed with books, some I recognize and others that are new to me. I see a worn copy of *Little Women* and warm to her immediately.

'You like reading?' I ask.

'Oh yes, I'm reading this at the moment.' She hands me a paperback, *Animal Farm*.

I read the back cover quickly. 'What's it like?' I put it on her desk.

'It's disturbing but I can't stop reading it.' She shrugs and pats the book. 'You can borrow it when I finish.'

A brightness opens up in my chest like a flower.

'You go to the American school, don't you?' she says. She has a slight American twang when she speaks which is very cute.

'Yes,' I reply.

'You're so lucky, I wish we had the money to go there. What are the boys like? Are they all gorgeous? Are they all foreign? Will you take me to one of your dances? They are supposed to be really cool,' she laughs.

'Where do you go?' I ask.

Bisi lets out a low groan. 'St Mary's Girls. It's awful.'

'Oh . . . sorry. Do you have dances?' I ask.

'Yes. They are OK. They invite the boys from the boys' school across the road. But I am sure they aren't as good as yours,' she says with a certainty that is hard to contradict. 'Are there loads of Americans at your school?'

'Not many, but there's a couple in my year. One of them is a boy who's half American and half Korean. And there's Judy.'

'Oh my!' Bisi shrieks. 'There's a boy I know who's half Korean, he is *gorgeous*. He's going out with one of my friends.' A loud squeal rings out through the house.

'What was that?' I ask.

Bisi's face turns serious and she lowers her voice. 'Oh. That's Mrs Ife's children. They're staying with us.'

'What happened to them?' I whisper.

'I think her husband beat her up and kicked her out onto the street. He took a second wife. My mum said she was found walking down the expressway, carrying all their things in plastic bags. The other Nigerwives went to collect the children while the husband was at work. Now he's looking for them. I don't know what will happen if he tracks them down . . . that's why they're trying to get them out of the country, maybe back to America but anywhere safe, really.'

'Oh my god.'

'Mrs Ife is in a bad way. She stays in the room all day. I don't think her family in America want anything to do with her because she married a black man . . . you know how it is . . .' She shrugs her shoulders and sighs.

I nod. 'Poor thing.'

'Lily!' It's Mrs Abiola.

'I think it's time to go,' I say.

Bisi grabs my hand. 'Wait. Write down your phone number.' She looks down shyly and I notice how thick and curly her eyelashes are – like a giraffe's.

'Of course. You give me yours too.' She hands me a biro and I scribble my number down while she does the same.

On the way home I ask Mum how she is going to help.

'I'll give them money and make some calls to book an appointment for them at the American Embassy.'

'Will they be all right?' I ask.

Mum stares out the window at a blind beggar holding his hand out at the car. He is gripping the shoulder of a little girl. She's wearing a stained dress with holes in the armpits. Mum rolls down the window and hands her a wad of cash. The girl passes it immediately to the man and they move on.

'I don't know. Her American family won't help. She'll be going back to nothing. We want to get enough money for her to live for a few months. She should be able to get a place to stay and some kind of benefit in the US. But it will be tough.'

Suddenly Mum turns to face me and takes hold of my hand. 'Never give up your life for a man, Lily.' She's quivering. Her jaw is set, mouth pursed. I glance at Peace in the rear-view mirror. His eyes meet mine and he smiles and gives a quick shake of his head as though to say, *don't mind her*.

*

The following weekend, Bisi comes round for the afternoon. When I show her my room, it's not my books she's interested in, but my wardrobe – she makes a beeline for the closet and starts pulling things out, holding them up to her body, striking poses.

'I heard you can wear whatever you want at your school.'

'Yeah … But sometimes that's quite a drag, worrying about what to put on in the morning.'

Bisi isn't convinced.

We're going to the Rec Club together, so we get changed. When Bisi puts on her bikini, I can't take my eyes off her bum.

'It's big, isn't it?' she says and bursts out laughing. 'It's so annoying, it just gets bigger every day. Soon I'll be able to serve drinks on it.'

I throw back my head and clap my hands. I haven't laughed so freely in years.

'You would be really popular in my school – you are so pretty *and* you're half American,' I say. It's true. More importantly she isn't awkward or gawky, she's got a confident way of moving through the world.

'Thank you,' she smiles.

When we get to the club, Bisi hones in on several good-looking expat boys messing around at the deep end of the pool.

'Do they go to your school?' she whispers.

I look over and recognize Bassim; he's with another Lebanese boy who doesn't go to our school.

My heartbeat races.

A few minutes later Bassim comes over.

'Hi,' he says and then spends some time allowing his eyes to travel down my body. I am wearing a blue bikini with padding in the bra. 'What are you up to?' he asks.

I shrug. 'Nothing.'

I glance over at Bisi. She is almost vibrating and her face has gone bright red.

'Who's your friend?' Bassim asks, smiling at Bisi in her frilly pink bikini.

I introduce them to each other and Bassim reaches over to shake Bisi's hand.

'Well, see you around, I guess,' he says and walks off.

'Oh my god! Did you see the way he looked at you? Oh my god! He was so cute!'

I laugh and lie back on my lounger. 'Yeah, but he didn't invite us over.'

'So what!'

'That's the big thing I hate about my school. There are all these rules about who can and can't hang out with who, who's cool and uncool – Bassim's in ninth grade, and I'm not rich or pretty or white enough to be popular, so there's no way he'd be seen socializing with me.'

'Oh god, it's like in the movies with all the drama!' gushes Bisi. Then she grabs my forearm and suddenly looks serious. 'Come on, stop feeling sorry for yourself. Let's go for a swim.' She stands and pulls me up and over to the water. I slip in and bob about, making every single move for Bassim's eyes only; and whenever I check over to see if he's watching, I'm pleased to find that he is.

After a while we go back to our sun loungers and each order a Chapman to drink and a plate of suya to share.

'Oh my god! He's still looking at you. Tell me again why you aren't going out?' says Bisi; she's holding a piece of suya with onion in her fingers.

I shrug my shoulders. 'I told you, I'm not cool enough.'

'That sounds silly. Why don't you ask him?' Bisi says.

'Me?' I point at my chest. 'No way. I could never ask a boy out.'

'Why not?'

'I don't know. I just couldn't.'

'Well, it's your loss.'

I glance over at Bassim, who's packing his stuff to leave. As he walks away, he waves bye to me.

*

A few days later I am sitting watching a film at home and the phone rings. I answer it.

'Hi Lily, how are you?' It's Bassim. He must have got my number from the school directory.

My mouth goes dry and I find it difficult to speak.

'Are you there?'

'Er yes,' I manage to say.

'I thought maybe we could just chat. So what were you doing when I called you?'

'I was watching a movie, *Apocalypse Now*.'

'Oh wow – that's dark. What do you think of it?'

'It's pretty disturbing but I couldn't stop watching it.' We chat like this for a while and then he asks if I'd like to meet at the club one day. I agree. When I put the phone down I have a warm feeling flowing through my body and I can't stop smiling. I wouldn't say I am in love with Bassim, he's shorter than me and very skinny, but I am happy that someone likes me, it makes me feel special.

The next day at school I bounce in and when I see Bassim I give him a beaming smile and wave as I walk towards him. But then I stop in my tracks because he isn't smiling at me, his face is hard and he's avoiding my eyes. He starts talking to his friend Rino who looks over at me and laughs. I grasp a fistful of air as I lower the hand I was waving and realize I must look like I am drowning. Hot liquid dread rises up from my stomach to my face and burns my cheeks. I turn around and go to my locker, hide behind the door and pretend to look for something.

I spend the rest of the day in a state of confusion, not understanding why Bassim would blank me like that. I try to get his attention discreetly when he's alone but he ignores me. By the time I get home I am frustrated and upset.

When the phone rings I rush to pick it up.

'I'm sorry about today, you know how it is . . .'

'No, no, I don't. I don't understand why you behaved that way.'

'I'm sorry, Lily. We just have to be different in front of everyone.'

Understanding begins to dawn on me with a painful ache. Bassim is ashamed to be seen with me. I slam the phone down. The next day at school I pretend he doesn't exist. When no one is looking he smiles at me and tries to catch my eye but I don't fall for it. He's a coward. He likes me but because I'm not cool enough he doesn't want to go public with it. And instead of feeling sad and helpless and ugly like I usually do when someone disappoints me, I feel powerful – like I finally have control over myself, over my feelings.

*

I am not remotely prepared for the day my cousin Chike comes to visit. When the doorbell rings, I go to answer it like usual, and standing in front of me is my dad. I blink a few times, shout for Mum, turn on my heels and run upstairs.

Eventually Mum comes to find me. She tells me off and instructs me to go back to the door immediately and apologize to my cousin – my *cousin*? – for my rudeness. I protest, tell her how was I to know, I've never seen him before; but she frowns so sternly that I know to back off.

Reluctantly I do as she says.

Back at the door, it's hardly less of a shock. This man really is the image of my father, but younger. In fact, the more I look at him the more differences I find. He's more dishevelled for a start, in a tatty old shirt and stained grey trousers, and his skin has a reddish hue as though he has been dipped in henna. Also, he smells. Instinctively, I don't like him.

'Chike,' my mother says gently, 'I didn't know you were coming. Come, let me get you some food and water. You look exhausted. Have you travelled down from Onitsha?'

'Yes, Ma.'

Mum leads him to the kitchen. There is something off about Chike. The way his red-rimmed eyes keep darting about the room, and how he keeps raising his left hand to tap his temple. He is muttering something under his breath that I can't understand. I think it must be Igbo. Mum calls the house girl Victoria to prepare some food for him and she pours him a glass of cold water. He gulps it down in one go, bangs the glass on the table and looks up at my mother expectantly. She pours him another glass and this process goes on until he has drunk four glasses of water.

'We'll leave you to eat, Chike, and when you finish come to the lounge.'

I follow my mother to the lounge and ask impatiently, 'What's wrong with him?'

'Lily. Listen to me. He is like your daddy was. He has the

242

same illness, and I think he must be off his medication. I wonder if his mother knows he's here. I will call her right now.'

'But what exactly is wrong with him? You told me Daddy was unwell when we were in Manchester but you never explained what that meant.'

My mum looks irritated. 'Now is not the time, Lily!'

'At least just tell me what this illness is called,' I press, certain that I am going to find out something important.

Mum blinks a few times and then sits down heavily on the sofa. 'It's called schizophrenia.'

'Schizophrenia,' I repeat.

My mum pauses, her eyes move away from mine and she nods. Then she goes to the phone and starts dialling. I focus on the door and sound out the word *schizophrenia* in my mind.

When Mum puts the phone down, it's just as she suspected. 'He stopped taking his medication a few days ago and disappeared last night. It's pretty lackadaisical of them not to inform the police he was missing.' Mum shakes her head and stands up.

'Wait – but what is schizophrenia, Mum?'

She lets out a huffing noise. 'I don't have time to explain now, Lily, I need to deal with Chike. It's a mental illness. It makes you see things that aren't there and hear voices.'

She moves towards the door.

'And that's what Daddy had?'

She nods.

'So what's going to happen now with Chike?'

'Well, his mother is sending Nkechi to come and collect him. She'll get here tomorrow.'

'So he's going to stay here, with us?' A pressure is building up in my ears and I can feel blood rushing behind my eyeballs.

'Of course, Lily. He can stay in the bedroom at the end of the hall. You don't need to be frightened, pet, he's harmless.'

I stare at her doubtfully. 'I'm staying in my room as long as he's here.'

'Lily,' my mother's voice is suddenly raised, 'don't be so unpleasant. He's your daddy's nephew, and his favourite one at that. Chike even used to live with us in Port Harcourt.'

I turn and run up the stairs.

Mum shouts after me and I can hear the rage in her voice but my fear of being near Chike outweighs my fear of my mother. I stay in my room for the rest of the day, think about my father and Chike and schizophrenia. I think back to all the times my father acted strangely in front of me. When he sat in his chair staring into space, as though he were watching something. The times when he would pace up and down, arguing with someone who wasn't there. And then I think about The Incident, when he was attacking my mother, and wonder if in fact he was seeing my mother at all or was it someone else he saw? And as these scenes play out in my mind, I feel a slight loosening in my chest because if schizophrenia is an illness that makes a person behave in a certain way – doesn't it mean that my father hadn't been a bad person? Doesn't it mean that he wasn't in control, that, in a way, he was possessed by something that made him do things he didn't want to? Like in that terrifying film *The Exorcist* where the girl is possessed by a demon. And then I think about how frightening that must have been for Dad. This causes a twisting feeling inside me as I imagine it. I put on my headphones to try to block it out. I close my eyes and let the rhythm of 'Running Up That Hill' by Kate Bush rush over me in waves. I am not quite soothed but the sensation of a hand pulling at my insides has stopped.

A few hours later I can hear Mum showing Chike to his room. Only when I am certain his door is closed do I open my bedroom door and tiptoe over to the room I share with Mum. Even if I now can name what's wrong with Chike, that doesn't make him any less dangerous. Mum is already changing for bed. She glares at me as I enter, her grey eyes glinting.

I sit on my bed feeling ashamed.

'You've been so rude, Lily.'

'But don't you understand, I'm scared of him. He reminds me of Daddy when he was sick.' Heat is building inside me. 'And you never explained what was wrong with Daddy. About the schizophrenia.'

Mum's expression softens. 'I'm sorry, Lily, I thought you were too young to understand then. It's all right, pet. It's an illness just like diabetes. It's just that it affects the person's brain so it makes them behave differently. They have to take medication to make them better but sometimes they don't take their medication. It used to happen with your father – he would have an episode, take his medication, get better and then feel like he didn't need the medication because the side effects were difficult for him. And then he'd end up sick again.'

She let out a sigh and then put her hand softly on my shoulder.

*

The next morning, still feeling a bit guilty, I have breakfast downstairs with Chike and Mum. He looks better, has had a wash and some rest, and I notice he is wearing one of my father's short-sleeved shirts and trousers – all of this helps me feel a bit less wary.

I watch him as he eats. His movements are much slower than Mum's, his eyes look dulled, and of course I remember this grogginess from seeing how Dad changed after he'd taken his medicines. Everything seems familiar, and yet I am understanding it in a whole new way. Chike is staring at the cup of Lipton's tea on the table in front of him, barely moving or even registering his surroundings.

'Drink your tea, Chike,' Mum gently encourages him.

His eyes slowly move to her, then look back at his tea and eventually he picks it up to drink.

Even though breakfast is less frightening than I thought now that he has been sedated with medication, the memories of my dad are too overwhelming for me to stay. I eat my toast quickly and return to my room.

A few hours later the front doorbell rings. It's my cousin Nkechi. I like her – she has a kind face and a wide smile and she always calls my mother Mommy. The last time I saw her was at Dad's funeral, at the graveside with Auntie Ada. I go downstairs to say hello. Today, she is wearing a buba made of green patterned material, a matching wrapper and headscarf. Chike is sitting near her on an armchair, staring into space.

'Ah ah! Lily, big girl like this! Ha! When you grow so much, Lily? Eh?' She laughs, and the joyful sound in our silent, sombre house makes me smile.

After the initial greetings, Nkechi turns and goes to her brother. The smile drops from her face as she speaks to him quietly in Igbo.

After a while Mum gestures her to the dining room and calls Victoria to bring lunch. My mum and Nkechi chat about life in Onitsha, Auntie Ada's health and the goings-on of all the seven other cousins.

When it comes time for them to leave, Nkechi stands up and taps Chike on the shoulder. While she says goodbye and hugs me and my mother tightly, Chike stands stiffly by her side. Eventually she takes his arm and guides him out to the waiting car – and I know that without her help, he wouldn't know how to move forward, let alone where to go.

As I watch them leave, a pain moves from my armpit and snakes across to my heart.

CHAPTER 30

Manchester, 1990

Something changed for me when I went into ninth grade. I had been relatively happy up until then. But my joy was a delicate thing, easily shattered by the tiniest touch. And in ninth grade someone came along and destabilized me. It was to be my last year at the American school and I don't know if it was because of this I became so obsessive, whether it was my need to cling onto the stability and happiness I had gained while being there. The idea of everything changing again, of having to start over in yet another school, was too much to bear.

Lagos, 1988

The thought of going into my last year at the American school is strange. At the end of last year, I thought ninth grade would be the best year ever. I was starting to feel like I fitted in and the fact that a boy liked me made me feel more attractive. But things changed yet again over the summer. My legs are too long for my body. My waist curves on one side and bulges on the other. There is an internal imbalance when I walk, as though I might topple over, and when I sit at the table I have pains in my back that make me slump over in my chair and hold my belly.

And then there's my hair. I cut it short in eighth grade and now it's a large Afro.. It's frizzy and dry and I hate it. So, to try to take control over some aspect of my body, I've decided to relax my hair. For ages Mum refused, saying I am too young, that it would be bad for my hair, that all my hair would fall out, that I'll have to wear wigs. When that didn't work, she changed tack, told me I don't need to do anything to my hair, that it's beautiful the way it is. Still, I don't believe her. Sophie relaxes her hair and *she* thinks it's the best thing I can do and eventually Mum has to relent.

On the day, I am more nervous than I thought I would be. Sitting in the chair, breathing in the strong chemical smell, I stare at my reflection in the mirror and tell myself to relax. First the hairdresser rubs thick cream onto my head. It feels cool – not as bad as I thought; actually quite refreshing. She continues applying the cream and then my scalp begins to prickle and burn; it starts at the back of my head, slowly at first and then increasing in intensity until it works its way across my scalp and my head feels like someone has poured acid all over it. I raise my hand and say, 'It's burning me.'

The hairdresser, a young woman with long braids, laughs. 'Eeee dey burn ehh?'

I nod vigorously and try to keep the tears that have formed in my eyes from running down my cheeks. 'It's too much!' I say breathlessly. My back is dripping with sweat and I notice my hands trembling.

'Make you deh wait small small or eee no go take.'

I close my eyes and breathe through my mouth because the smell coming from my head makes me want to throw up. All I can picture is my hair falling away from my head in clumps as it's washed. I grab the hairdresser's forearm and beg her to take it off.

'Oyinbo! No for fit take pain like Naija gal!' The rest of the customers burst into laughter.

'I can't bear it any more!' I wail and press my nails into my palms.

'OK, come, come.'

She leads me to the sinks. Cold water pours over my scalp, bringing a sweet relief. It still stings raw in places, though, as if the skin has burned away. She wraps a towel around my head and takes me back to the chair. Then she unwraps the towel and stands behind me, watching as I stare at myself in the mirror. My hair is shiny and straight, just like Sophie's. I can't stop smiling and clapping.

'Ehhh? You dey like am now!' says the hairdresser.

She puts in rollers and sits me under a dryer and when she pulls the rollers away, my hair is bouncy and glossy and sleek.

And for the first time, I'm actually looking forward to going back to school.

*

On the first day of the new school year, I walk to the lockers in the morning feeling like everyone is staring at me. Meera runs up to me looking puzzled. 'Yael *told* me you did something, er, *different* to your hair.' Meera sniggers into her hand.

I try to ignore it, asking her how she spent her summer, but I have a sinking in my belly.

In class, I'm introduced to Jane, a new girl from England, and at recess I go over to where she's sitting alone eating a sandwich.

'Hi, I'm Lily, can I sit?'

She nods.

'What part of England are you from?' I ask.

'Kent, it's in the south.'

'Ah . . . My brother and sister live in Manchester.'

'Oh, that's in the north. I've never been.'

As we are chatting, Ngozie, Ifeoma and their clique come over and stand around Jane, ignoring me entirely.

Ifeoma smiles her cutest smile and flutters her eyelids. 'Welcome to the American school, it's so lovely to meet you. Would you like to come with us? We can show you round.'

'Sure,' says Jane, gathering her things. 'Aren't you coming, Lily?'

Ifeoma narrows her eyes. I am definitely not invited.

'No, you go ahead. I'll see you later,' I say.

To my surprise, after recess Jane comes over to find me in class.

'God, those girls are awful! Can we have lunch together tomorrow? OK?'

After that we become friends. Jane isn't particularly pretty, with her thick frame, her brown hair cut into a short bob and her ordinary clothes – khaki shorts, plain tops and trainers; but she is cool in other ways. For a start, she knew Ngozie and Ifeoma are super-bitches in an instant and has no interest in trying to gain their favour. Also, she knows lots about music. Sharing the earphones of her Walkman with me, she introduces me to bands I've never heard before – The Cure, Joy Division, The Smiths. She tells me two of the bands come from Manchester and I almost feel a little proud to have lived there.

*

One day, I ask Jane more about her old school back home.

'It was OK. I've been in boarding school since I was five.'

She gives a twisted smile and scratches a mosquito bite on her leg. Her legs are covered in them. We sit in silence for a few minutes, the quietness hanging heavy between us until – to my relief – the bell rings and we go back to class.

There's an air of melancholy that hangs around Jane. It makes me want to be around her because I think maybe she's also been through some difficult times. She's quieter than other girls, more thoughtful; she is also extremely clever. It's not just the fact that she always gets the best marks and seems to breeze through the weekly pop quizzes set by the teacher while everyone else struggles at their desk. She seems to understand the nature of things, why people behave the way they do. Nothing gets past her.

One day she says, 'The kids at this school are all idiots. They are all living in a bubble.'

I ask her what she means.

'It's hard to explain, this whole situation is fake. These kids are only here because the companies their parents work for pay the fees. In their own countries they'd be nobodies. There are only one or two actual Americans and yet everyone tries to act American, as if we're actually *in* America. But they aren't and we aren't!'

Jane turns to me and gestures with her hands. 'Look, in England anyway and I guess probably in the States, being "cool" isn't about trying to be something you're not. It's about being confident enough to be exactly who you are, an individual, different, a person with their own thoughts and style and taste. An original.' She paused. '*Nobody* here gets that. Apart from you, I think, deep down.'

I feel like I'm glowing.

'The problem is a lot of kids are just acting a part. Most of them are too spoilt and silly to be cool,' she explains.

I nod, finally understanding.

'What you're saying is, everyone should just be themselves.'

*

'I don't like any of the boys at this school,' says Jane.

'What about Nick?'

'Him! God no, he's all brawn and no brains.' Jane laughs.

As we are talking, a boy called Dele walks past. He's half Nigerian and half Guyanese.

'He's not bad,' she comments.

'Who?'

'Him, Dele in our class.'

I can't hide my shock. I know Dele quite well because he also lives in Apapa and sometimes I give him and his little sister a ride home.

'He's got such beautiful skin and he's funny and clever.'

In all my time at the American school I don't think a white girl has ever openly liked a black boy, apart from Astrid, but Michael was very fair skinned. My respect for Jane grows even more.

Dele doesn't belong in any particular clique. He brags a lot to the girls about how great he is at sports and this makes him a bit comical, strutting round like a cockerel. Ngozie and Ifeoma both like him, though, and are always trying to get his attention – which, of course, he loves.

He hardly speaks to me at school, beyond a quick nod and smile across the classroom, but away from school, Dele is actually quite different. He's far more sensitive than anyone realizes. I see Segun and Nick low-key bully him most days and how, as soon as he closes the car door to come back to Apapa, he relaxes a lot and tells me all about the girls he likes and what idiots the other boys can be.

*

Dele is overjoyed when I tell him Jane likes him – but from the strength of his reaction, and all the things he confides to me about Jane, I'm not sure she likes him quite as much as he likes her.

To act as go-between, I tell Dele to come and join us on the steps one day at recess, which he does, and when he and Jane are settled into their conversation I go to the library and leave them to it.

At class Jane tells me they are a couple now. Just like that. Their relationship causes a predictable scandal. People just can't understand – he is black, she is white, he is uncool, she is cool – but Jane and Dele don't seem to care. They spend every free moment together . . . and I'm back to being alone. For the first time ever, I have something in common with Ngozie and Ifeoma – they want Dele to split up with Jane; and I want my new friend back.

I've never seen Dele so happy. There's a light in his eyes and when he's holding Jane's hand in the corridor he seems several inches taller than his actual height. But as the weeks go past Jane seems to grow a little indifferent.

To my surprise, and secret delight, she dumps him after a month.

'He's just a boy. He doesn't even know how to kiss properly. Not that there are any *real* men at this school anyway.' Jane shakes her head.

'I know what you mean,' I say, not knowing what she means. 'Why don't you come to the Apapa club with me one weekend? There are loads of Lebanese boys there. They are all gorgeous.'

Jane's face lights up.

On his part, Dele doesn't take the breakup well. During our car ride home, he's in tears.

'I don't understand what I did wrong,' he wails.

'Don't cry, Dele,' says his little sister who looks worriedly at her big brother.

'That's because you didn't do anything wrong, Dele,' I say. 'Look, I really don't think she was the right girl for you.'

It's hard watching Dele cry. His face is moving around like a pond in the rainy season and it strikes me how childlike he is. I feel bad for him. I recognize that pain of heartbreak, of being tossed aside like a dirty rag.

'I'm so sorry, Dele. Do you want to come round and watch a film? You can choose.'

'No, I'm too depressed.' He stares out the window at the Lagos traffic and doesn't speak for the rest of the journey.

CHAPTER 31

Manchester, 1990

I developed an unhealthy obsession with Jane. I was possessive and jealous if she even spoke to anyone else. I clung to her like she was the last life boat on a sinking ship. I'm not sure why I was so intense about her. I think it's because she seemed to be the only person at school who saw the real me and still liked me. Unlike my siblings before, and my mother and all the other kids in the American school, Jane thought I was worth spending time with.

Lagos, 1988

Mum has always warned me to stay away from the Lebanese boys at the Rec Club. She claims they will 'ruin a good girl's life'. I think about Bassim and how he wanted to ignore me in front of other people. Maybe Mum is right but it's difficult to pull my eyes away from those boys, they are all so good-looking with their green eyes and dark hair. At the Lebanese video shop, the boys behind the counter chat to me eagerly and while I always behave as if I'm not in the least bit bothered, I love feeling the delicious tingle on my skin as their hopeful eyes follow me around the store.

Truth be told, I don't much like the Rec Club in Apapa. It is small and badly maintained. Once I went for a swim in the pool and among the debris I encountered in the water was a beer bottle and, to my disgust, a fried egg. When I got out, my skin had a layer of grease that took a lot of scrubbing with a loofah to remove. But I've told Jane I'd take her, so off we go.

Jane has loaned me one of her bikinis, white with graffiti writing on it in various colours. We lay our towels on the sun loungers and Jane looks over at the pool.

'Don't go in. It's filthy,' I say.

She shrugs and rifles around in her bag, pulling out a packet of cigarettes and a box of matches. She puts a cigarette between her lips, lights it and closes her eyes as she inhales deeply. A plume of grey smoke emerges seconds later. She offers me the pack.

'Do you want one?'

I must have a shocked expression on my face because Jane laughs and says, 'Don't look so *frightened*, Lily. Have you never tried smoking before?'

Suddenly I feel as if I'm being childish.

'Go on, try one, you'll never know what it's like if you don't.'

I hesitate before taking a cigarette and placing it between my lips. She lights a match and I lean in for the flame.

'You need to inhale,' she says.

I take a strong puff; smoke fills my lungs and nose. I cough and splutter.

Jane laughs.

I try to smoke like I've seen movie stars do. But it doesn't work. The whole experience is disgusting.

The only other person at the pool is a woman with a toddler.

'Where is everyone?' Jane asks.

'They might be in the hall.'

'Let's go, then!'

Jane jumps up and starts pulling on her shorts.

'I don't know ...' I say weakly. I'm uncomfortable with the idea, as the hall's always full of boys, never any girls.

'Come on ...' Jane hauls me to my feet.

The moment we enter all the boys look up from the snooker tables, as I knew they would. I shrink back but Jane sidles over without a hint of shyness and asks if we can join them.

'Of course,' says a boy who looks vaguely familiar from the video shop. 'I'm Ramzi.'

'I'm Jane, and this is my friend Lily.' Ramzi ignores me.

Jane gestures me to come and join in the game, but I don't know how to play and don't want to seem stupid so I sit on a nearby chair and watch as Jane moves around the table, the boys completely enthralled by her confidence, her ease.

As the boys crowd around my friend, I start to panic. Nothing about this room, this gang of boys, feels safe. I have to focus on the floor to try to breathe evenly.

'Are you all right?' Jane is standing in front of me.

I'm relieved to see her. 'I think I need to go outside for a minute.'

She looks concerned but also a little irritated to have to interrupt her fun. 'Sure. You go, I'll wait here.'

I rush out into the garden. It's late afternoon and the mosquitos are starting to wake up. I lean against a banana tree, breathe in and out slowly and close my eyes. I check my watch, it's only 5.30. Peace isn't due to pick us up till 6 p.m. Eventually, reluctantly, I go back in and order a Coke at the bar.

At 6 o'clock, I have to find a way to get Jane's attention. I move towards her, trying to catch her eye, but she ignores me.

'Jane,' I say in a low voice. She looks at me impatiently. 'We have to go. Peace is waiting.' She rolls her eyes but starts to say her goodbyes. Phone numbers are exchanged. Once we are in the car she is back to her normal self. She chatters away about the boys, especially Ramzi. I listen and nod and mutter encouraging words, but I am glad when we finally drop her off.

As Peace drives me back home he says, 'Dat girl no good. Eh dey make am trouble fah you.' He shakes his head.

An unsettled feeling has lodged itself inside me, a premonition of something bad. I distract myself by taking out a tissue from my jeans pocket, tearing a small piece off and rolling it between my fingers until it becomes a ball. Then I push it under my fingernail until the pain blots everything out.

CHAPTER 32

Manchester 1990

Jane triggered all my mother's protective instincts, although I didn't see it that way back then. Instead, I thought my mother was trying to ruin my life. I had finally found a true friend, the person who gave me what my mother couldn't, and it seemed like all she wanted was to take that away from me. I was so angry with her.

Lagos, 1988

Jane lives in a flat in Ikoyi. Her mother, Mrs Hewitt, is just serving us dinner when Mr Hewitt arrives home. He has white hair and small blue eyes rimmed with white eyelashes.

His skin is so pale I can see the veins on the backs of his hands.

He greets me as he joins us at the table. In front of us there is a pack of cream crackers and some triangles of cheese on a plate.

'Go ahead, Lily.' Mrs Hewitt smiles and gestures towards the crackers.

I take a few and some slices of cheese, feeling awkward under Mr Hewitt's gaze. Jane is very quiet during dinner.

'Where are your parents from?' Mr Hewitt asks me.

'My mother is Irish, and my father is . . . was Nigerian.' I trip over my words. 'He passed away a few years ago.'

'Oh, we're so sorry for your loss,' says Jane's mother.

'I didn't realize,' says Jane, looking hurt. She rarely asks about my family life and I don't volunteer information so I feel as if I've done something wrong.

'And you've lived here all your life?' continues her father.

I nod, deciding not to go into my time in Manchester in case he asks me why I lived there.

I have finished my crackers and cheese and I don't think any more food is coming. I reach for some more and immediately Mr Hewitt gives me a disapproving stare.

'You know it's rude to come to someone's house and eat all their food.'

I stare at my plate ashamed and not sure what to do. Jane has gone bright red. I've suddenly lost my appetite.

As soon as we are allowed to leave the table, we rush to Jane's room. She throws herself on the bed.

'He's such a bastard. I hate him. I'm sorry he spoke to you

like that, Lily. He was probably rude to you on purpose because you're my friend. I can't wait to leave home.'

'Oh, don't worry, it's all right,' I say.

Jane often talks about leaving home and I find it a little shocking how fiercely she longs to grow up. She's always talking about the future as though it's a country she can't wait to move to, whereas the idea of facing the world as a grown-up terrifies me. Right now I want things to stay as they are. I hate the idea of change.

When I get home I tell Mum all about the evening.

'Well, what do you expect?' she says triumphantly. 'The English! They are so stingy!'

*

Once the girls discover that Jane is hanging out with boys from outside school they find her newly interesting. Yael in particular, who has ditched me as her class partner and has started joining me and Jane at lunchtime. It's making me really anxious because I am used to being shoved to the side for someone better, so I'm waiting for it to happen again.

Ifeoma and Ngozie seem to have a personal vendetta against Jane. The Dele situation didn't do her any favours and they hate her even more because she is better than them academically, having knocked them both off the top spot. The school has formed a new student-parent-teacher committee. We have to vote for student representatives and it's no surprise that Ifeoma and Ngozie get voted in. No one else particularly wants the job.

One of the first things they do is to make a complaint about Jane – saying that she is introducing 'unsavoury characters' and 'bad influences' to the school. Jane brought Ramzi and a few of his friends to a couple of school dances, which nearly caused a riot, all the girls vying to get to dance with the handsome older boys. A couple of them were caught smoking in the corridor and Ifeoma and Ngozie jumped on this as a perfect example of why the school should ban anyone who isn't a student here from attending future events. A letter was drafted and sent out to all parents and students. Jane laughed when she read it. She doesn't seem to care. If it were me, I'd be mortified by that campaign of hate.

*

If Mum was concerned about Jane's influence before the letter, after reading it she doubles down on her warnings to be careful of 'that English girl'.

'Going around chasing Lebanese boys and she's only fifteen!'

'Jane is the best friend I've ever had, Mum!'

Mum leans forward.

'*I'm* your real friend, pet. Trust me. A girl like that is bound to get you in trouble.'

'Mum! You haven't even met her!'

'OK, OK. Look, how about you bring her over? Let me judge for myself.'

'Next weekend? There's a party nearby so she can stay over.'

'A party? Whose?' Mum looks suspicious.

'I don't know, a friend of Jane's. It's all right, Mum.'

'I'm worried about you. I know what a delicate little flower you are. You're soft and sweet, and that's wonderful – but there are plenty who like to take advantage of good people like you.'

*

Jane and I are in the car on the way back home to get ready for the party. We're stuck in traffic and, to make it worse, the air conditioning isn't working. Mum is in the front with Peace and I can see the sweat pooling on the back of her neck, damp patches on her shirt collar.

The usual traders and beggars weave in and out of the traffic. A leper comes up to Mum's window, a gaping hole where his nose should be, completely eaten away by the leprosy. He holds a fingerless hand out. Mum slaps her newspaper against the window and shouts, 'Get away!'

The beggar moves quickly on to the next car. Jane remains silent for the rest of the journey.

Shame spreads into my stomach. Mum has never shooed away a leper before and I know she has been generous to that man on several occasions. It seems to me she's acting like this to make a point to Jane. My shame turns to anger.

As the traffic eases we start moving, driving alongside the lagoon. In just a few months the smooth surface of the lagoon has become covered with tangles of green plants. I watch as a fisherman tries and fails to row through the bushes. I know from my Biology classes that the ecological balance in the lagoon has changed. Something is causing the overgrowth.

When we arrive home, Jane hops out and looks around the garden and house in surprise.

'Your house is huge, Lily,' she says.

I rush to show her my bedroom and start to get ready for the party. Mum is hovering in the corridor.

'Hello, girls. Don't mind me. I just wanted to ask Jane about this party. Whose is it?'

Jane looks up at my mum, and it strikes me how young she appears.

'Her name is Emma. She's an English girl.'

'I see. And do you have her parents' number?'

'Yes, I wrote it down somewhere.' She starts rummaging in her bag, seemingly flustered under my mum's scrutiny. The silence that follows is unbearable.

After a few minutes Jane admits defeat. 'I might have to call my mother and ask her.'

'Yes, will you do that, please?'

Jane nods but doesn't move.

'Off you go then, the phone is downstairs.'

I'm so embarrassed as Mum follows Jane to the phone and watches her as she dials.

'You'll need this.' Mum hands her a pen and a notepad.

Eventually Jane gets through to her mum and writes down a number. After she puts the receiver down, she hands the notepad to my mum, who says, 'Thank you, Jane.'

We go back up to my room and shut the door.

'Jesus, your mum's like a school marm,' says Jane.

'Who's Emma? And what if Mum actually calls her, like, before we even leave?'

'Don't worry. She won't. And Emma's a friend – I'll just have to call her when we get there and tell her the story so we're all clear.'

I'm so angry with my mother for causing all this trouble with Jane. For highlighting how strict and uncool she is.

There is a knock on the door. It's Mum.

'Jane, I called the number and I spoke to Emma's mother and she doesn't know anything about a party and neither does Emma.'

All the blood in my body seems to rush to my head and a dizzy feeling comes over me. I watch as Jane's face turns from pink to bright red. Her eyes study the ground in front of her.

My mother's face has hardened and her eyes narrow. 'Look, Jane, I can't allow you to take Lily to this party. I don't know who is holding it and who will be there. I'm afraid you can't go.'

Jane looks up at my mother; their eyes meet and Jane opens her mouth then closes it. My mother glares at my friend before turning and leaving.

Heat is rushing through my body and the dizzy feeling has come back. A combination of fury and humiliation rises in my chest.

'I'm so sorry, Jane.'

Jane sits on my bed and stares at the wall in front of her, then she looks up at me.

'Your mum's a complete bitch, Lily.'

I nod vigorously. 'I know. I hate her.'

CHAPTER 33

I thought that Jane was going to be my salvation, that being around her would make me special, loved and worthy. I was ready to throw all my love and devotion into Jane, to do anything to make her happy. But I wanted something in return: complete loyalty and to be her best friend. And when she didn't behave in the way that I wanted her to, that's when things started to go wrong.

Lagos, 1989

Cracks are appearing in our friendship. It started with the cancelled party. When we went back to school after that weekend I sensed a difference. A coldness within her. She was less attentive to me; when I talked to her she nodded and made small noises but her eyes were always searching for something around the room.

Then, over Christmas she went back to England with her family and I spent two weeks in a state of agitation, wondering if she'd still be my friend when she came back in January.

It's the first day back at school in the New Year and instead of just walking with me between classes she has asked Yael to join us. This makes our duo an awkward trio. I would have thought Jane wouldn't want the competition – Yael's far cooler and prettier than either of us – but clearly I'm wrong.

Now we always walk three in a row, Jane in the middle and Yael and me on either side. I feel increasingly like a spare part, yet I can't stop following her around like a dog. I can't let her go, even though I know it's all going to end badly. I hate myself for it.

At recess, Yael pulls Jane aside and tells her to come for lunch with her Israeli clique.

I turn and watch as they go off together, so shocked I can't even move. Finally I grab my lunch and walk in the opposite direction. I find a private place to sit where no one can see me crying. They just completely ignored me.

Back in class, Jane comes over to me looking concerned.

'What's wrong, Lily?'

'Nothing,' I say and get my book out, hoping the teacher isn't late so we can just get on with the lesson. I have to control my breathing so I won't burst into tears again and really humiliate myself. I must already look like a mess with my puffy eyes and swollen lips.

I don't even bother trying to walk with Jane and Yael to the next class.

*

To my surprise, at lunch the next day Jane comes and sits with me.

'Yael's such a vain cow. I went to her house the other day – she's got photos of herself plastered all over her room.' She sniggers. 'Who does that?'

I can't believe what she's saying about someone who seemed like her new best friend less than twenty-four hours ago . . . It freaks me out a bit but I am pathetically grateful that she is sitting with me today. Then, she starts to tell me all about her trip to the beach with Yael at the weekend. It's the first I've heard of it, and knowing they have been excluding me, perhaps for some time, makes me want to cry.

'You should have seen the bikini she wore, Lily, everyone was staring, it was practically a *thong*. You should come with us some time.'

From wanting to cry, to wanting to sing!

And just like that, Jane is my friend again . . . for now.

*

It happened again, as I knew it would but hoped it wouldn't. It was at the dance. The three of us were dancing in a circle to Belinda Carlisle's 'Heaven is a Place on Earth' – but by the end of the song, Jane and Yael were holding hands, laughing, and somehow I was dancing on my own.

After a while I shrank away to the bathroom. I don't think

Jane and Yael were ignoring me intentionally – they were just lost in their bubble of friendship and familiarity. They are both more comfortable in themselves than I am. The moment I sense that I'm on the outside, I am completely lost. Socially awkward, ill at ease with myself. I'm so terrified of losing the safety, reassurance and acceptance of my friends' approval that I can't just relax and have fun. The truth is, had I just joined in with them they probably would have let me. But I couldn't. I am too afraid of rejection. I need them to want me, to pick me, to give me permission to be me.

*

Ramzi has broken up with Jane. She can't believe he's ended things and asked me if I can get Peace to drive her to his place after school. I tell her it's a bad idea, but she begs and I finally agree.

When we get to his house she hops out of the jeep and rings the doorbell. I stay in the car and watch nervously as Ramzi's mother opens the door. When she sees Jane standing in front of her she shouts and waves her hands.

The mother is in a frothing rage.

'Get out!' she screams.

Jane holds her ground.

'You beta call am your friend, Lily,' urges Peace.

I go to Jane and lightly touch her arm. She's shaking and crying but she lets me lead her back to the jeep.

As we drive back I try to comfort her, with lines I've heard in movies or magazines. 'He wasn't worth it', 'You'll find someone much better' – but I know it's all just words.

'I slept with him, Lily. He told all his friends. I'm so embarrassed. He made me out to be some kind of . . . some kind of slut.'

'Well, what kind of a guy does that? He's only making himself look bad,' I say.

This doesn't help as she sobs louder and presses her face against the window glass.

I decide to keep quiet for the rest of the ride so I don't make things worse. Although I am sad that Jane's so upset, a small part of me feels like perhaps this is karma – now she knows what it feels like to be dumped by someone you love.

Not only has Jane lost Ramzi, she's lost Yael too – they got into a row; the Israeli and Lebanese cliques don't get along at the best of times and when she found out that Jane slept with Ramzi, Yael wants nothing more to do with her.

There was always a sadness to Jane. That's what drew me to her in the first place, but now it's like she's empty, like part of her personality has been erased. She no longer laughs or makes jokes or even bitches about other girls. Most of the time she just wants us to listen to music together.

For the first time in our relationship I am the one with the power, because I know I'm the only one she wants to be around.

*

When Mum hears about all the drama, she is unsurprisingly unsympathetic.

'I could have predicted that myself,' she says with a smug look that makes me angry. 'And what do the parents say?'

'I don't know. I don't think she talks about that kind of stuff with them.'

'Typical. Did you say they sent her to boarding school when she was young?'

'Yes, she was just five.'

'Shocking!' says Mum as she raises a hand to her collar-bone.

'Anyway, Jane invited me to Tarkwa Bay on Sunday with her family. Can I go?'

Silence.

'Mum?'

'No, Lily. You may not. That girl is no good and you'll be tarred with the same brush.'

'There's no fear of that. None of those boys are interested in me.'

'All the better. And anyway there are such dangerous currents at Tarkwa. It's not safe in the water. And there are huge barracuda there; I read a man was bitten the other day. No, Lily.' She presses her lips together.

I am furious with my mother but even angrier at myself for telling her about Jane.

'That's not fair!' My voice is raised and I notice my mother's face tightening. 'You're ruining my only real friendship! Just as you always ruin everything!'

'Lily, that girl isn't your friend. *I'm* your friend. I only wish you could see that.'

Something explodes in my head. 'What? You? You ignore me most of the time! If you were a real friend and mum to me I wouldn't have to go chasing after Jane!' I can't look at her because I'm scared I've gone too far.

I think back to how I was abandoned in Manchester, how

even when I came back, Mum's attention was always on Dad. I bite my lip and glare at my mother.

Her face darkens and her lips tremble. She looks down at the floor as she speaks. 'Lily. I know things haven't been easy for you, all the changes you've been through.' She glances up at me and then back at the floor. 'And it's my fault. I know I haven't given you the attention you deserve and I just ... I tried my best with you but everything with your father just got on top of me ...' She bursts into sobs. She holds her head with both hands and rocks back and forth.

'I'm sorry, Mum ... I didn't mean to upset you.' I kneel beside her, and the sight of her crying causes something to break inside me. She grips my hand tightly.

'I'm going to do better, Lily, from now on.' She meets my eyes. 'It's OK, Mum, I know you will.'

We sit like that and Mum's sobs subside until there is just the sound of her breathing. And even though this moment is painful and distressing it is also beautiful because my mother's love for me is radiating out from her – a warm feeling is filling me up and I want to hold onto it forever.

*

A few days later as I follow Jane to our usual lunch place she turns round. Her face is hard. 'I want to be alone, Lily.'

'What do you mean?'

'I just feel like being alone.'

My heart rate speeds up. 'Have I done something to upset you, Jane?'

'No, Lily, I just need some space. You're always in my face.'

A cold shiver runs up my spine.

'I'm just trying to be a friend.'

'A friend?' Jane gives a nasty laugh.' You don't think I can see how happy you are now that Ramzi's dumped me and Yael is ignoring me. You're so possessive, Lily! It's suffocating!' Her voice is raised and people are looking.

I step back as though I've been slapped. 'But, but what, what do you mean?'

'You don't think I see how jealous you were when I was friends with Yael, in fact when I even speak to anyone else? It's like having a jealous boyfriend. You want to control *everything*, who I speak to, who I'm friends with. It's disgusting, Lily.' Jane gives me a look that makes me want to hurt myself, to set myself alight and burn.

I run away, to the furthest corner I can find, then curl up into a ball and wail. The pain is not so much from Jane's words but from the realization that she might be right. That I am too possessive and that I just wanted her all for myself and I hated that she had other friends. It makes me a bit sick inside. What is wrong with me? Why am I like this? These questions swirl around my mind. I don't go back to class, instead I hide there until just before home time and then I grab my things from my locker and slip out before the bell goes. Thankfully Peace is early.

CHAPTER 34

Manchester, 1990

The breakup between me and Jane was painful but it highlighted some important truths to me about myself. I was too needy and controlling in my friendships. I think it's because I was insecure and unhappy in myself. I felt like if I didn't have that one person to love me that I was no one, that I didn't even exist in the eyes of others. I'm better than I was but I still tend to be needy. I haven't really managed to fix this. I'm trying to work on it by making friends with many different people. That way if one dumps me it's not so bad because I've got others.

Lagos, 1989

Things between Mum and me improved after our big argument. It isn't so much that we changed overnight. I just feel closer to her, like a wall of unvoiced hurt has been knocked down between us. We spend more time together. Sometimes I look at her as she watches TV and think this is all I have ever wanted – my mother is mine.

I keep my distance from Jane. She still speaks to me and is friendly but after our big blow up things are different. There is a weariness between us. And the funny thing is I am all right about everything. We don't hang out together any more, I go off on my own and she spends a lot of time in the library studying for her GCSEs as she plans to take them when she goes back to England.

Something else has changed too. I start to feel less awkward about voicing my opinions at school, rather than simply trying to second-guess what people want to hear. Anyway, we are almost at the end of ninth grade – we'll all be moving on. Though in my case, I'm still not sure where to.

Mum and I have talked in circles about the options. Despite all we've conquered, how much closer we've become recently, she still wants me to go to boarding school in England, like Maggie and Luke. But the very idea of going back there sends me into a panic.

'I don't want to leave you again, Mum.'

'It will be different this time, I promise. You are fifteen now; you know the schools here are no comparison . . . you have to get your education no matter what. It's what your daddy would have wanted.'

'That's not fair!'

'Look, Lily, you'll have Luke – and Maggie. We'll find a way, don't worry. You won't be all alone.'

I know there is no other way forward.

*

Jane left a week ago. When we said goodbye we held each other in a tight hug for a long time. We both promised to write – and I will – but as I watched her leave, I felt a surprising weight lift from my shoulders. No more pain or confusion. No more worrying about being left out. All I have to do now is get through junior high graduation.

For the ceremony, I have chosen a gold organza dress with silver trim embroidery around the edges of the sleeves and collar. As I walk into the hall with Mum and Sophie, I even feel pretty.

Ngozie and Ifeoma arranged the seating plan so obviously all the 'popular kids' – themselves included – are at the main table with their families. I don't really care. After a while, Mr Barry, head of ninth grade and my favourite teacher, stands and makes his way to the stage.

'Ladies and gentlemen. Some of our students have prepared a speech for today. So without further ado, let's begin. Lily,' he gestures to me, 'the student committee have chosen you to start the proceedings, so please come up. The stage is yours.'

I'm dumbstruck. Nobody mentioned anything about a speech. I press my nails into my palms to distract myself from the wild galloping of my heart. Ngozie and Ifeoma can barely contain their smirks. With all eyes on me, I stand up shakily and don't feel my legs walking to the stage. At the microphone, standing there, in front of that sea of faces, a feeling of complete abandonment comes over me. It reminds me of the time I got lost in Manchester. My body tenses as I search my mind desperately for something to say. Sweat starts to course down my spine in rivers.

Mr Barry comes to my side.

'Lily, we want to congratulate you on graduating from our school. You've finished the year with an excellent 3.8 GPA.' The audience claps loudly. My mind is completely blank. I try to steady myself by clenching my fists and pressing them into my thighs. But I still can't think of a thing to say.

'Is there anyone you want to thank, dear?' prompts Mr Barry. 'Perhaps you'd like to thank your mother . . . '

I close my eyes for a moment and listen to my heart thudding in my ears. I take a deep breath to steady myself and a memory pops into my head – of a little girl marching into the principal's office to complain about being bullied by a teacher.

I open my eyes and say, 'Yes, I'd like to thank my mother, for all her love and support. Thank you, Mum.' I look over at Mum and we both smile.

'Well, that's fantastic, Lily, thank you!' He nods and takes the microphone.

'And we can see this beautiful young lady is destined to become one of those super models we hear so much about. Look at how lovely she is.' He claps and then leans in close to me and whispers, 'You're fine, honey. Go and sit down.'

I return to my seat, relieved but happy.

The next person to take the stage has clearly prepared for the occasion, and he reads out a long speech that makes the audience laugh and applaud. When it's Ngozie's turn, her speech lasts a full ten minutes.

Maybe moving to England isn't such a terrible thing after all. A new school will be a fresh start for me. I might even find a boyfriend and make new friends. I will miss Mum but she says she'll come and join me in a year's time, when she has her pension. I can do this. I've done it before and survived. Nothing could be worse than the first time I lived in Manchester.

EPILOGUE

Lagos, 1990

It's the first time we have all been together in Lagos since Dad's funeral. We are here for the five-year memorial. We gather around the grave. I'm holding a bouquet of fake flowers. We decided this is better than real flowers because they just die and dry up after a couple of days in the African sun and there's nothing more depressing than dead flowers on a grave.

My mother is standing next to me and Sophie is on my other side with Fela and their baby girl. Maggie is heavily pregnant, clutching her English husband's hand. Luke is with his new English wife Kelly. Peace stands respectfully a little away from our group, hands held together in front of his body, looking down at his shoes.

We are silent as the Irish priest says a prayer. I think about my father and how we were all affected by his illness. Each of us dealing with it in different ways; my mother with her alcohol, pills and anger, my brother Luke running away from home, my sister Maggie also staying away and turning her back on her roots. And then there's me, with my insecurities and possessiveness. The only one who doesn't seem as affected is Sophie; maybe that's because she is the oldest and she knew the man Dad was before. I move closer to my mother and grip her hand tightly.

I wonder how things would have turned out if my father hadn't been ill. Would all of us have been different? Happier? I don't know. Maybe I would have been a better person, more confident, more at ease in the world. But then again I wonder whether, in fact, the opposite is true . . .

As we walk away from the grave I listen to my family talking. Mum is complaining about the state of the graveyard, how it hasn't been looked after. Luke suggests we all go for a meal at Federal Palace Hotel. Everyone agrees. Once we pass through the gates of the graveyard it's as though something has lifted. I feel lighter.

ACKNOWLEDGEMENTS

This book would not be out in the world without my wonderful agent Jessica Craig who believed in me and continues to champion my work. Thank you, Jessica! I want to thank my publisher Sarah Castleton, who not only gave me a chance but also helped untangle all my knots and shaped this work into what it is today. Thank you to Tamsin Shelton for her fantastic copy-editing. I want to thank the team at Atom Books including Stephanie Melrose, Francesca Banks, Phoebe Carney and Olivia Hutchings (who helped me through my very first workshop at YALC). I would like to thank Ellen Rockell for the beautiful cover design.

This book started off as random scribblings and if it weren't for the helpful critiques given by my writing group on Scribophile I'm not sure it would have become a novel. Thank you to Dawn Miller, one of my first readers.

Thank you to Emily Critchley and Amy Baker for their feedback on an early draft. I want to thank the author groups Debuts 2021, 2022 and the UK YA authors support group.

Thank you to my family, my sister Anne for her encouragement and answering all my questions about the past and giving me ideas when I needed them. Thank you to my niece Alexis and her partner Leroy for their help with 1980s Mancunian slang and Jamaican patois. Thank you to my partner Damiano for his encouragement and belief in me and for reading an early draft. Thank you to my mum who, when I wanted to give up or when I faced rejection, constantly encouraged me and told me to keep going, that it would happen one day.